ALMASI SHEIKHS

The Sheikh's Contract Fiancée

The Sheikh's Unruly Lover

The Sheikh's Pregnant Employee

THE ALMASI SHEIKHS SERIES

THE SHEIKH'S
Pregnant Employee

LESLIE NORTH

BLURB

All it takes is one night of passion to change your life forever.

Layla's trip to the Middle East started off with a bang. Amid the sultry heat and exotic luxury of Dubai, she shared a single night of passion in the arms of a sexy stranger. Layla can't say she regrets it, until she walks into her new HR job and comes face to face with her one-night stand. She never thought she'd see the sinfully handsome sheikh again, but his icy reception makes it clear he wants nothing to do with her. Zahir Almasi is equal parts infuriating and irresistible, but Layla won't make the mistake of falling for his charms again.

Sheikh Zahir Almasi has been groomed since childhood to be a dutiful son. Now that he's assumed his role in the family company, it is one he takes very seriously. So when the seductive American he slept with walks into his office, Zahir is stunned. He can't let Layla distract him from his path—no matter how enticing she is. But the more they work together, the less he can deny their attraction. The Western beauty may not be a suitable woman for him, but Zahir can't help but wonder if he'll ever be satisfied with just one night.

As their appetites for each other increase to an undeniable level, Layla discovers a secret that changes everything—a secret she isn't sure she ever wants to share. Layla is pregnant…and Zahir is the father.

Thank you for purchasing 'The Sheikh's Pregnant Employee'
(Almasi Sheikhs Book Three)

Leslie North is the USA Today Bestselling pen name for a critically-acclaimed author of women's contemporary romance and fiction. The anonymity gives her the perfect opportunity to paint with her full artistic palette, especially in the romance and erotic fantasy genres.

Get SIX full-length novellas by USA Today best-selling author Leslie North for FREE! Over 548 pages of best-selling romance with a combined 1091 FIVE STAR REVIEWS!

Sign-up to her mailing list and get your FREE books:
leslienorthbooks.com/sign-up-for-free-books

For all books by Leslie North visit:
Her Website: LeslieNorthBooks.com
Facebook: www.facebook.com/leslienorthbooks

TABLE OF CONTENTS

CHAPTER ONE

Layla peered out the window from the backseat of the sedan. Her friend Marian had warned her that coming to Parsabad would be not just entering a different country, but a whole different dimension. Private cars, lush suites, a celebrity family...Layla blinked down at the seat under her, dragging her fingertips over the leather. It was softer than crushed velvet.

Welcome to Parsabad. After a direct, eight-hour flight from New York, she was both exhausted and excited. Time to get this trip started off on the right foot—with friends, laughter, and plenty of exploration.

Because this was more than just a vacation to come see her best friend Marian get married. This was also the start of a year-long excursion around the world.

Per Parsian wedding protocol, Layla's pad for the next two weeks would be something like a penthouse suite, according to Marian. All of the family members of both sides coming from out of town would stay in a block of rooms at a swank hotel in downtown Minarak, but Marian had scored Layla the crème de la crème. To celebrate her pending travels, Marian had said, where surely she'd be forced to sleep in bunk beds in questionable hostels with questionable sanitation standards.

Excitement prickled through her. There was so much to discover about Parsabad. She'd never been to this part of the world, nor any of the neighboring vicinities. It served as the perfect launching point for her year off from work. Start with Parsabad, move on to Egypt, then cross over to Greece, which would launch her European leg of the tour. From there, who knew. She would go where the wind took her.

The car pulled into a cul-de-sac circling an enormous fountain flanked by sculpted mermen and sirens creeping out of the stonework. The water blazed bright red and orange, reaching nearly a story in height. As the driver unloaded her big backpack from the trunk, Layla gawked, her gaze moving from the ostentatious water display to the shining behemoth hotel before her, glinting silver and steel for what seemed like miles into the sky.

"Are you sure this isn't Dubai?" Layla had never been there, either, but what she'd seen of Parsabad so far seemed a lot more like the world-famous megalopolis. The driver gave her a tight smile as he handed over the pack. She slipped him a tip and then strolled into the hotel, feeling exactly like an important jet-setter with the whole world at her fingertips.

The inside of the hotel gleamed like freshly polished gold. In fact, that probably *was* gold lining the walls, and each panel of the floor, and the spiral columns arching up toward an atrium ceiling where birds twittered. A rush of water sounded from

2

somewhere—maybe this was also a science museum in addition to a five-star hotel. Layla approached the receptionist's desk, unable to hide a goofy grin.

"I'm Layla Kirk." She slid her passport across the marble countertop. "Guest of the Almasi Wedding Party." She waited to see if this would elicit any coos or acknowledgement. The receptionist did look mildly impressed, which was good enough.

"Yes, miss, we have your reservation here." The dark-haired employee clicked around on her computer, and then grimaced. "I have a note from…Marian?" She tripped over the first name. "It says here to call her as soon as you can. There was a delay in their return trip."

Layla's eyes widened. "Okay. Thank you." Marian and Omar had taken a romantic getaway, but should have been back by now.

"Here is your key. Take those elevators to the top floor." The receptionist pointed toward a row of elevators along the far wall and smiled primly. She was so beautiful—almond-shaped eyes, jet black hair that looked heavy and silken. Pretty much everyone she'd seen in Parsabad so far was gorgeous. It gave her hope for a proper Parsabad welcome.

Because there was one thing on Layla's to-do list, above and beyond helping her best friend celebrate holy matrimony to her love. Layla wanted a sexy, foreign hook-up. A one-and-done night overseas with someone she'd never met before, someone she'd never meet again.

Once she got to her room, suite 903, she slid her keycard into the door, holding her breath as the door swung open. The room had a *foyer*. In NYC, she had a tiny studio. She stepped inside tentatively, gasping as her gaze landed on each new fascinating thing: a white-brick fireplace, a wall-to-wall window overlooking downtown Minarak, a balcony with a legit *hot tub* on it. The bedroom of the suite was bigger than her apartment back home, easily. She flopped onto the bed, face first. *I want to live here forever.*

She pushed up onto her elbows, pulling her cellphone out of her pocket to call Marian. Her friend must be thanked for pulling whatever insane strings required to snag this room. And Layla needed to see what exactly "delayed" meant.

Marian picked up on the second ring. "Are you in Parsabad?"

"You bet your ass I am." Layla rolled over onto her back, staring up at the gauzy fabric of the canopy. No detail was overlooked in this suite. "I just checked into my room and…I can't even begin to describe how luxurious this is. Marian, this is bigger than both of our apartments combined back in the city."

"I know," Marian gushed. "I knew you would love it. Consider it our 'Welcome to Parsabad' gift. And I'm even more relieved now, since Omar and I are trapped out of town overnight."

"Oh. Is that the delay? Is everything okay?" Layla bounced her leg against the mattress. It sprung surprisingly high into the air.

"Yeah, but our flight got cancelled coming back into Minarak, so we opted to just stick around for another day." Marian let out a dreamy sigh. "I can't complain, either. It's been so nice to get away from work and all the wedding planning."

"Well, let me know if I can do anything until you get back. As your bridesmaid, it's my duty."

"You just stay put and relax. And take a taxi tonight to go have some drinks! One of our favorite clubs downtown is called Echo. In fact, I would have taken you there tonight myself."

"Hmmm." Layla smoothed her hand over the bedspread. Shimmery green and like silk. "That sounds like a fine idea. *And* I'll let you take me there again once you're home."

"Perfect. And just text me if you need anything tonight. You know, questions, translation issues, if you get lost on your way to Echo…"

Layla laughed. "I think I got it covered, girl. But I'll let you know if anything comes up."

The two hung up the phone, and Layla lay back on the bed, stretching out with a smile. There was no better way to start this trip: a full bank account, luxurious surroundings, and a totally empty evening in front of her to fill however she pleased.

Hours later, the night was unfolding like the most unexpectedly beautiful bloom. Perfect outfit—a skin-tight black dress with black heels—followed by a perfect meal—eggplant and exciting sauces—and now, a taxi to Echo for the perfect way to finish the night.

She paid the taxi driver and blurted out the politest thank-you she could manage in Farsi, and strutted up to the front door. There was a little line, but she was ushered to the front door immediately. *Thanks, Little Black Dress.* She'd hadn't even needed to drop the Almasi name.

Inside, the lounge was moodily lit with upscale bars sweeping along glass-blocked walls. Every bartender had a suit and tie on, as did many of the male patrons. Maybe this was why Marian and Omar liked it—it was the corporate crowd getting their fix.

Layla ordered a gin and tonic, thankful the bartender spoke English, and then retreated to the sidelines to absorb the scene. Lo-fi electronic music pulsed through the speakers, and a stage area was hidden behind drawn, black curtains. Round tables dappled the room. Lithe, pristinely contoured ladies leaned toward model-worthy men, everyone the definition of dark and mysterious. A shiver ran up her spine. Maybe this would be *her spot* in Minarak. A lounge without the nightclub raucousness. Perfect for classy yet alcohol-fueled encounters.

She slid into a seat at an empty table, eager to people-watch and relax. There was something comforting in hiding behind a wall of music. It acted like a buffer, a filter through which she could peer at the world—and men—around her.

Her gaze gravitated toward a man across the room, leaning against a smaller bar near the stage area. He was dressed in the standard business-class uniform—dark, tailored suit with shiny leather shoes—but something about his stature drew her in. He didn't just stand tall, he blasted confidence. Even from across the room, something about the way he moved his hands and leaned against the bar told her he'd be a fantastic storyteller...or maybe a huge asshole.

Interesting. Noted. Layla scanned the room, sipping at her drink. Alcohol sizzled through her veins, and she cocked a grin. Already this vacation was so *fun*. Even if it involved simply observing sexy men and fantasizing about them later, it was a glorious departure from the routine of her former corporate life.

The man across the room looked out over the lounge area as if he owned the place. Maybe he *was* the owner. His gaze flicked over Layla and then returned a short moment later. He held her gaze from across the lounge, his eyes dark and smoldering. The corner of his lip turned up, and Layla couldn't look away to save her life. She only hoped she wasn't drooling into her gin and tonic.

She blinked, trying to regain some control over her brain, and sipped again at her drink, offering up a coy smile. *Dear lord, if he comes over here...* A moment later, he pushed off from the bar and headed her way, his gaze set on her like a target, his steps measured and casual.

Oh my god. She tossed back the rest of her drink and pushed the glass away, smoothing her hair. She practiced a neutral expression, something midway between disinterested and too-cool-for-school.

"You must not be from around here."

Layla tilted her head back to look at him. His voice was husky velvet, his gaze commanding as he watched her. He rolled a tumbler between his fingers as he awaited a response.

"Maybe, maybe not." Did that count as coy? Across the sea, who knew what the rules were. She crossed her legs, allowing a length of thigh to slip into view. His gaze darted downward and his grin widened.

"May I sit with you?" He gestured toward the open chair.

"Please." Her heart hammered between her ears. *Play it cool.* She could be courting a billionaire, for all she knew. Some guy with a private jet and a thousand casinos. "How did you know I spoke English?"

He slid into the open seat, his gaze never leaving her. Cologne wafted toward her, something exotic and spicy. "It was a wild guess. Thought I would have a better shot speaking English with a foreigner than Farsi."

"You have a point." She bit back a grin. "So you're from here?"

"Born and raised." His English had a distant British lilt, like maybe he'd learned in a boarding school. "But I don't think the same is true for you. Are you passing through?"

"Yes, unfortunately. I mean, not unfortunate that I'm here. I love that I'm here. But rather, that it's so brief." She forced a smile. The man made it impossible to *think*.

His grin widened. "What brings you here?"

I thought it had been my best friend's wedding, but maybe it was to meet you. "Just traveling around for a bit. I'll start here, move west and then north." Why are you so hot?

He hummed low, as if assessing the route. But even that rang sexy and slightly animalistic to her. Like maybe that sound might pair equally as well with pushing her up against a wall and having his way with her.

"An exciting trip. How long will you be traveling?"

"Oh, about a year." It felt good to say it—even better when his eyes rounded with admiration.

"That's quite some time. What a noble journey. I'd be lying if I said I didn't think about trips like that myself."

"You should take one, then." She shrugged. *Come with me, why don't you?*

He smiled mysteriously, his gaze raking her up and down. "That's a fair suggestion. What's your name?"

She had to catch her breath before she answered. "Layla. And you?"

"Zahir." He held out his hand, and she took it hesitantly, like maybe there'd be a static shock. But instead of a zap there was only incredible warmth, a smoothness that begged her to feel every square inch of this man. Her breath hitched. "It's a pleasure to meet you."

"Likewise." Their grip lingered too long. Definitely too long. She couldn't look away from him—it was like he'd roofied her only with his gaze. When their hands finally slipped apart, his lips quirked up in a secretive smile.

"May I buy you a drink?"

She shook her head. "Do you wanna get out of here?" The words flew out of her mouth before she could even think otherwise. Hopefully the dimness of the lounge would cover the blush in her cheeks. Zahir straightened a bit.

"I'll follow you anywhere you take me."

His words melted over her like butter on a hot stove. She pushed to standing, unsteady on her own two feet as she practically floated out of the nightclub, clutching Zahir's wrist behind her. If this wasn't the fastest pick-up in all of history… Something about this man just demanded it. *It's okay for things to be about sex sometimes. Especially when the guy you're inviting back to your all-expenses-paid penthouse suite looks like he commutes to work in a helicopter and Gucci underwear.*

She made a note to look at his underwear brand in the penthouse. Pushing out into the warm air of the Minarak evening, Zahir turned to her, his jaw impossibly square. In the comparatively quiet air outside, he looked somehow even more perfect. As if every last hair on his head was individually styled.

"I've called my driver. He'll take us wherever you'd like to go." His warm hand appeared at her waist, drawing her near. She inhaled sharply, pressing herself against him. Heat rolled off of him in waves, nearly drowning her in his scent.

A few moments later, the car pulled up. Zahir held the door open for her and she slid into the backseat. Remarkably similar to the car that had picked her up from the airport, but maybe that was what all the top-end sedans were like here. Zahir, too, had something familiar about him. A distant impression of Omar, but again—she was probably just seeing similarities between the only two Parsian men she knew.

The car ride was quick, but they descended into making out even quicker. His lips were salty and warm against hers, needy kisses sparking like a forest fire. Heat prickled through her, sending her senses into overdrive. When the car pulled up to the hotel, she could barely detach from Zahir's face to make it out of the car.

Outside, he smoothed down the front of his suit coat, looking toward the hotel. "Nice place."

"Yeah, I'm staying here for a while." She grabbed his hand, leading him inside. She couldn't have hidden her smile if she were forced at gunpoint. Zahir played it cool, and when she sidled up to him in front of the elevators, he stiffened.

"We should wait until we're inside your room," he whispered hotly into her ear. He squeezed her hip, which sent a lightning bolt of pleasure down to her toes. "What I want to do to you shouldn't be seen by others."

Her thighs clenched involuntarily. She looked up at him to say something, but her voice had shriveled.

"Cameras follow me occasionally," he added.

"So you're a celebrity." Inside the elevator, she waited for the doors to close before she pressed her lips against his. Celebrity status made him even hotter. They kissed fervently until the elevator dinged on the top floor. She pulled him by the wrist toward her suite and nudged open the door with her hip. Once the door clicked shut behind them, he pressed her against it, dragging his tongue slowly up the side of her jaw.

"Oh, my god," she said, her voice shaking.

He laughed gutturally and slid his hands down the sides of her dress, hooking palms beneath ass cheeks. He hoisted her without any hesitation or effort; their groins made a hot seal.

"God, you're sexy," she whispered, pressing her head against the door as his kisses skipped hot and juicy over her jawline, down to the crook of her neck, over the exposed cleavage.

"Not as sexy as you." His voice was a strained murmur, as if it might break into a moan at any moment. He ground his hips against hers, the pronounced hardness meeting the anxious nub between her legs.

She clawed, nipped, and lunged for him, desperate to feel him inside her, desperate to reach that peak with him. Their lips met jerkily, haphazardly—distracted kisses amid the groping and disrobing. Zahir stumbled toward the bed with her in his arms, his pants around his ankles, and then she was bouncing on the silky bedspread, wriggling out of her dress.

A moment later, she heard the rip of a condom wrapper, and then he flipped her onto her belly. She arched herself up to meet him. Finally the hot press of his groin, the slow and slick entrance, followed by shuddery moans that only grew more gravelly the deeper he went.

Zahir moved against her in a rhythm both desperate and slow. She relished every second of it as he cupped a breast in his big hand, his face buried in the back of her neck, his pelvis rocking her closer and closer to ecstasy.

The orgasm came swiftly and powerfully. She fell over the edge way before he did, but that only meant she came a second time when he finally tumbled after her.

As they lay panting in the aftermath, eyes sparkling and chest heaving, Layla couldn't feel anything but pleased with her first night in Parsabad.

CHAPTER TWO

Zahir tapped a pen against his desk, trying for the millionth time to focus. Two executives had been at each other's throats for weeks now, and today, of all days, it had finally escalated to him.

On the exact day when Zahir couldn't use his brain for anything except recalling images from his sexy night before.

Layla flashed across his mind's eye again—the tousled strawberry blonde hair he'd tugged from that chignon, letting it spill over lightly freckled shoulders. Her skin had been creamy, like a pudding dessert. He'd certainly licked her all up—not just once, but almost six times. They'd had to abandon the sixth attempt due to exhaustion and his impending work day, but they hadn't lacked the willingness.

He hadn't had that many orgasms in one day since his college years.

"Zahir?" The voice on his phone's speaker brought him back to reality. Zahir blinked guiltily at the executive sitting in front of his desk, then squinted at the telephone.

"Yes. Excuse me. I was thinking." *About Layla.* "These issues have been getting worse, haven't they?"

The executive director in front of him widened his eyes. "He refuses to follow the etiquette guidelines I've emailed to him."

Zahir looked toward the phone. The American counterpart was on the line; these two employees had similar roles on either end of the world and frequently had to work together. But social—and cultural—clashes continued to erupt between them. And as Zahir poked around in other departments, he found similar clashes erupting on a smaller scale.

"I can't be expected to change my approach just because he sends me an email," the American colleague complained. "That's not policy. That's not *protocol*."

"But it's *reasonable*," insisted the Parsian counterpart.

Zahir sighed. He could see a long future of these sorts of conflicts, but how to resolve them? It seemed both sides were equally staunch in continuing their own status quo. "As you both know, there is no other option beyond working together on this."

"I know—" began the American colleague.

"But he's been so—" started the other.

"And I think the best way to formally address this issue, which will continue to crop up, is through policy." He paused, rolling the pen between his fingers. He'd been catching whiffs of Layla all day. How was that even possible? It threw him off balance. "And I think we'll need to bring in someone who can help train, educate, and mediate precisely these types of issues."

His mind kicked into overdrive as he felt the pieces of a solution clicking into place. "For now, however, put aside your frustrations and find a way to work together. You're both going to have to give a little. I'll let you know when we have a formal next step in place."

He dismissed the Parsian colleague and said a curt goodbye to the American on the phone. And then he headed straight for his father's office to present a plan that seemed more and more like the inevitable solution.

"Father." Zahir burst into the large, dimly-lit office, his father barely looking up at him. Omar sat in a chair in front of the desk and turned with raised eyebrows. "I have an idea that I need you to approve."

"Hardly much choice, is there?" His father removed his glasses, rubbing at his face before appraising his eldest son.

Inwardly, Zahir scoffed at the comment. His entire life had been one big lack of choice. His future had been eternally prescribed by the man in front of him. As the eldest Almasi son, Zahir's destiny was firm: take over the business, be the head Almasi once their father passed. And while his brothers had different weights to bear with their own stations inside the family, Zahir was unequivocally the only one who was *trapped* by the expectations.

And he'd shouldered this responsibility because it was expected of him. Because it was the right thing to do. Because he valued his family more than anything else in the entire world.

"This must be a good idea." Omar sat up straighter, crossing an ankle over a knee. "Do share."

"These repeated and incessant culture clashes cropping up, on both sides of the ocean," Zahir began, leveling his family members with his gaze. "It's gotten to the point where productivity is being impacted. We have to curtail it and *solve* it."

"Agreed," their father rumbled.

"I think what we need more than anything is a bridge between the two companies. Parsian or American—it doesn't matter. Just someone trained in Human Resources with enough sensitivity to help us combat these issues and develop policies to handle them," Zahir said.

Omar nodded slowly. Their father glared at Zahir as he spoke, but it was just his thinking face.

"It can be a temporary position or long-term. Let's think of them as a cultural sensitivity trainer, someone experienced in reacting to the needs of *our* company straddling two very different social realities." The words flowed easier for him the more that he spoke. "But more than that, they will be the point person for handling these issues. It frees us up from dealing with these quarrels like elementary school teachers. We can all focus on our tasks, remain productive."

"Brilliant," Omar murmured.

"Hmmm, yes." Father replaced his glasses. "Have you looked at budget?"

"We have enough," Zahir said. "It would be a salaried job, yes, but simply one additional spot."

"I know someone who might fit the bill," Omar said.

"Yes?" Zahir steepled his fingers, pleased by the reception, but more than that, his spot-on delivery. When he was on, he was on.

"Marian has a friend with a spectacular HR history. A stellar resume overall. Plus she travels; she'd be a perfect fit for the job."

Zahir shrugged. "Get her in here. Is she New York-based?"

"Normally. But she's actually in town now, here for the wedding. I bet we could get her in for an interview."

Zahir nodded, Layla flashing through his mind's eye. She was the only American he cared to think about after last night. That hook-up had practically burned their clothes right off.

"She has preference, then," Zahir said, pushing to standing. "Seems like she's part of Marian's chosen family, if she's traveled here for the wedding, and that works perfectly for our family business model. I'll inform Mr. Thomas of our plan, as well, since it affects both divisions."

Zahir squeezed his brother's shoulder on his way out of the office. Some days—moments like these—he was okay with the task of leading the Almasi family, of steering the business eventually. Even though he hadn't chosen it.

Back in his own office, Zahir slid back into his chair, mind wandering immediately to Layla. He hadn't felt such a visceral *lack* from not being around someone before. They'd been together a total of six hours before he'd snuck out of her hotel and back to his own penthouse early that morning, but today every cell in him screamed for her, like a petulant child seeking candy.

It wasn't fair. Especially since he hadn't gotten her number or any other form of contact.

The only ideas that came to him were visiting the club again…or showing up at her suite. Though a surprise visit sounded a bit intrusive. He *could* call the hotel, leave a message for her with his number. Something simple, seductive, and easy.

He was dialing the hotel's number before he could even register the fact that he'd made the decision. The phone rang twice before a receptionist answered.

"Hello, I would like to leave a message for suite number 903." Zahir paused as the receptionist readied to take his message.

"Please write, 'I can't stop thinking about you. I need to see you again. Yours, Z.'" He relayed his phone number to her, and then hung up the phone, satisfied.

This way, the ball was in her court, but she knew exactly where he stood.

Now all he had to do was wait. His eyes drifted to his phone, as if maybe a call would come through instantly. The anticipation would be nearly too great to bear.

CHAPTER THREE

Layla smirked over top of her latte. Marian couldn't see through her sunglasses just how smug she was, but her friend would know something was up.

"Spill it. You're hiding something from me." Marian sounded wry as she sipped at a glass of water. This was almost like back in NYC at their favorite spot, if only she looked past the fact that everyone around them spoke Farsi.

"I hooked up with a stranger last night." Layla giggled despite herself. It wasn't the most scandalous thing for a twenty-nine-year old woman. But it sure was *fun.*

"A Parsian dude?" Marian didn't seem shocked, but she sure sounded intrigued.

"Oh yeah. Like, *the hottest Parsian dude.*" Layla sighed, sitting up in her seat. Her body still ached from the marathon sex-a-thon the night before. Her pussy might take a week to recover. But if given the chance, she'd do it all over again that very night if she had the chance. *Except he left me with no way to find him ever again.* That was the rule of the hook-up. One and done. Exactly what she thought she'd wanted.

Except she wanted to see Zahir again immediately.

"Damn. That was fast." Marian took a bite of her sandwich, chewing thoughtfully. "Is that why you didn't mind a late lunch?"

"Yeah. I had to get *some* sleep last night." Layla sipped at her latte. She'd ordered some biscuit-y looking things and some sort of soup, but she wasn't quite hungry yet. Her body only wanted Zahir. "I need to be fresh for my day of sightseeing."

Marian's face fell when Layla had expected the opposite. She creased a brow. "I thought you'd be a little more excited about that."

Marian paused, nervous gaze skating over her face. "I am excited for you. I just…I have to tell you something."

"Oh god." Layla's stomach shrank to a nut. "If this is about the wedding—"

"No," Marian blurted. "Nothing of the sort."

"Good. Because if you and Omar split up I'll kill both of you." Layla pointed her finger at Marian as threateningly as she could muster.

Marian relaxed, a full grin blossoming on her face. "It has nothing to do with that. I just…Omar brought up an idea today that he wanted me to pass along to you."

"Okay." Layla sipped at her latte again. It tasted distinctly different, but she couldn't pinpoint how. "Lay it on me. Omar is an idea man; I like what he comes up with."

"Well…he wants to hire you."

Layla furrowed a brow as the word struggled to fit together in her head. "He what?"

"This is why I was hesitant to tell you. I know you're launching this big trip, and you've been so excited for it…but Almasi-Thomas established a new position, and you'd seriously be *perfect* for it."

Layla blinked, pushing her glasses up onto her head. "What?"

Marian grimaced. "I know the timing is bad. But maybe it's actually perfect. You wouldn't have to do it for long. But they need someone *now*, and you were practically born for this job."

Layla narrowed her eyes. It smelled and sounded like a trap. "You want me to rejoin the corporate world."

Marian sighed. "God, you make it sound like a prison sentence."

"I just *quit* the corporate world!" Layla took a heated bite of her biscuit.

"I know. I know. But seriously consider this. The money would be great, and you'd be set up to travel even *longer* afterward. Turn your one-year trip into two or maybe even three years."

Layla stared at the table as she chewed, mulling over her friend's words.

"Once you get everything up and running, you can slip away and keep moving on. This will just be a temporary layover in Parsabad."

Layla swallowed, the idea percolating in her mind. It was sounding less and less awful. But maybe Marian was sugarcoating it.

"You've been trying to get me to work for this company for years," Layla said. "And the second I get to Parsabad a position opens? This is probably part of your sinister plan." She scoffed, taking another bite of the biscuit.

Marian grinned wryly. "This is no sinister plan. But it would be *amazing*, Layla. Come live with me for a little bit in Parsabad. It doesn't take you that far away from your goal, which was to get out of the States and travel. Now you can get to know Parsabad *really well*, and then continue on from here. Exactly the way you planned."

Layla narrowed her eyes. "How much money?"

"A lot." Marian cleared her throat. "Omar and his brothers will discuss that with you when you go in for the formal interview. And just think—everything you earn here goes to *travel*."

God, Marian knew all the right things to say. Extra money didn't hurt. And she wasn't entirely opposed to the idea of padding her bank account via a sweet gig abroad. Really, there was a spark of excitement in her. Starting a corporate job in a foreign country was still exotic and new. Just slightly different than she'd imagined it.

"This is a good move," Marian insisted. "And they need someone stat. Please, Layla. Do it for me. We can hang out all the time and go to shitty movies and drink wine every weekend."

"Ugh. Those are all of my favorite things." She gulped back the last of her coffee. The position intrigued her, despite the fact that it put her right back into the working world. "Fine. But only if you stop *begging*."

Marian squealed, and then clamped her hand over her mouth. "Yay! I knew you'd come around."

Layla sighed, melting into her seat. "God. This means I have to go shopping for work clothes. I just got rid of all that shit."

Marian squeezed her hand. "I'll take you out tonight after work. I know exactly where to find the cutest stuff. And trust me, the fact that you, me, and Annabelle will be work colleagues is going to take corporate life to a whole new level. These Parsian men won't know what hit them."

A grin flickered over her face. Okay, so the idea wasn't all bad. She just hadn't expected to settle down so soon. Like 48-hours-after-take-off *soon*.

"The brothers want to meet with you tomorrow," Marian said, dabbing at her mouth with a napkin. "I'll give them the good news today, then I can bring you in with me tomorrow morning. Sound good?"

Layla's brows shot up. There went her relaxing first few days in Parsabad. "Dang. On the job so soon?"

"It's best to get the process started. You'll just go have the interview, get all the details, and then you can negotiate from there." Marian gathered her purse and the check, which she'd offered to pay. "I gotta go, though. I'll come pick you up after work."

Marian blew an air kiss and hurried toward the front of the outdoor café, where she paid the bill before scurrying off. Layla sat in a contemplative silence once she'd left, observing the other patrons, trying to get a feel for what an extended stay in Parsabad might feel like.

She couldn't deny it. There were tingles of excitement, despite the contractual obligation that came with it. And though it made no sense, she hoped Mr. One-And-Done from the night before might make another appearance in her life now.

Later that evening, after an admittedly rushed afternoon of sightseeing, Layla returned to her hotel to meet Marian for their agreed-upon shopping spree. The receptionist called her over when she passed by the front desk.

"There's a message for you." She slid a piece of paper across the counter, and Layla received it with a furrowed brow. In sloppy writing, someone had transcribed, "I can't stop thinking about you. I need to see you again. Yours, Z." Then a phone number.

Her breath hitched, and she rooted around in her purse for her phone. *Hell yes!* Mr. Mysterious was still enamored. Or at least lusting after her. She hadn't thought of anything but his luscious kisses all day.

Once she got her phone flipped around right, she fired off a quick message to the number on the note. *"Why hello, Mr. Z. Long time no see. It's been nearly 12 hours since you left my room."*

His response was swift. "12 hours too long. When can I see you again?"

A grin consumed her face and she clutched the phone to her chest. A love affair wasn't such a bad way to open up her extended stay. She drifted toward the lounge area, typing out a response. *"Maybe tomorrow. I'm booked up tonight."* Didn't want to seem too eager, even though her nerve endings had fired up when she saw his words.

"I'll be waiting."

When she looked up, Marian was heading her way, a brow arched severely. "Why do you have that look on your face in the middle of the hotel lounge?"

"Lover Boy wrote back," Layla gushed. "Or I should say Lover *Man.*"

"Mmm. You found a Parsian man so *quickly.*" The two headed out the main doors toward a taxi. Marian once told her that she insisted on doing things the regular-person way when she wasn't with Omar, to stay connected with her non-celebrity-business-family roots. "Is it wrong to want to meet him? You don't introduce your friends to one-night stands."

"Two-night stand," Layla corrected, excitement blooming inside of her. "There's definitely going to be a second occurrence. And I cannot freaking *wait.*"

CHAPTER FOUR

Layla zipped and bounced around the hotel breakfast area like she'd mainlined caffeine. Really, she hadn't even had a sip of coffee yet, but her nerves for the approaching day had her rattled in a big way.

Well, it was that and *Zahir.* They'd stayed up a little bit too long the night before with sexting and then outright sex talk over the phone, which ended with Layla fingering herself at Zahir's request until she came. The orgasm had been *almost* as powerful as the ones from the other night, which was worrisome. The man held some sort of sexual power that she was slowly and steadily succumbing to.

Not that she minded. At eight a.m., she fought to not text him. Even though every cell in her body was dying to start their messaging off bright and early.

Marian strutted into the hotel lobby, waving at Layla while she talked to someone on her cell phone. Layla grabbed a lavash flatbread and to-go coffee—more of a ritual from back home than anything, though she usually ate a muffin or bagel—and hurried after Marian. Her friend's conversation was short and professional.

"Right. Right. Well, we're on our way, so be prepared. See you in about fifteen." She swiped her phone closed, then hugged Layla.

"Who was that?"

Marian slid into the backseat of a taxi, and Layla followed suit. "Oh, it was Imaad. They're just getting ready for your interview."

"Imaad." Layla blinked, struggling to place the name. She couldn't think past any name but *Zahir*. "Oh, Annabelle's husband!"

"Right." Marian clucked her tongue. "Another fine specimen of the Almasi gene pool."

Layla snorted. "Finer than your own representative?"

"No, mine is the finest. And the eldest specimen isn't so bad, either."

"Oh, there's a third one?" Layla's gaze wandered out the window as they talked, taking in the golden hues falling over the sleepy Minarak. At this hour in NYC, the city would be bustling and noisy. Here, it looked like people were still only considering making their way to the office.

"Ohhhh yes. The only eligible bachelor. And, well, if you weren't going into an HR position, I'd suggest you get on it. But once you take the job, that option will be out, since he'll be your boss."

Layla sighed. "Well, I guess I'll have to be content with my hot Parsian stud, then. Poor me."

Marian nudged her side. "Yeah, I totally pity you. The Almasi family is kind of absurdly hot, though. Even Daddy Almasi, if you're into older, slightly authoritarian men. So consider yourself warned."

Layla huffed with a laugh, enjoying the cool lick of the morning air that crossed her forehead. "You make this sound like I have something to worry about."

"Well, every NYC girl who's joined the Almasi Holdings ranks recently has ended up marrying one of them." Marian's eyes twinkled.

The two laughed, and soon they pulled up to Almasi Holdings' building. On the way inside, they chattered about the upcoming wedding. Less than two weeks away and almost everything was taken care of. Marian seemed relaxed for a bride in the final days, but having so much money at her disposal probably helped things.

"Welcome to the Almasi Headquarters." Marian swept her hand in front of her as they strode through the expansive lobby. Pristine, white tiles gleamed underfoot; the walls were shiny like stainless steel, something both elegant and industrial reflecting back at them. There was serious money and aesthetic here. Layla took it all in as they headed for the elevators.

"I'll drop you off at the board room so you can meet the brothers and Mr. Almasi," Marian said, checking her wristwatch. "Once you all talk things over, I'm sure you'll sign the contract and get an office and all that fun stuff."

"Oooh, my office." Layla grinned as the elevators swooped upwards, her belly twisting. Meeting the Almasi family had a special weight to it, even though she already knew Omar. However, she only knew the romantic Omar, the Omar who'd contacted her with a desperate plan to stop Marian from leaving his life, the Omar who'd flown across the sea at the drop of a hat to surprise his love in Manhattan.

With their family empire, she assumed in the workplace things would unfold a little differently. At least more formally.

At the top floor, Marian led her down a carpeted hallway lined with closed, wooden doors. She stopped in front of one, her hand on the doorknob.

"Here we are." She grinned, tucking some of her curls behind her ear. "Go get 'em, tiger."

Marian pushed the door open, revealing a crisp, white board room. Natural sunlight poured in from the wall lined with windows. A long table filled the room, dotted with empty chairs. Except for four chairs near the head of the table. *The Almasis.*

Layla swallowed a knot of nervousness and shut the door behind her, trying to take it all in. There was Omar. He stood, as did the others, to greet her. Her gaze skated over Almasi Senior—definitely distinguished, but not her type. Then Imaad, far more sly and collected than she'd gathered from photos.

And then there was the third one. Her gaze traveled over Zahir's face, registering a stricken look, one of quiet panic, and then realization began to sink in.

Zahir. That's freaking Zahir.

"Welcome, Layla!" Omar swept toward her, pressing a kiss to her cheek. "We've been waiting for you."

Zahir is the third one. Disbelief made painful rounds in her head, and she could barely rip her eyes off of him. She forced a laugh, welcoming Omar's greeting, trying to jerk her brain back into a functioning mode. Zahir, the man who'd gotten her off last night when he whispered a breathy "I want you to come with your fingers inside yourself, imagining it's me."

She blinked hard, shaking each man's hand in turn. When she got to Zahir, electricity snapped through her. *Please don't blush or fuck this up.* She'd already slept with her boss—what a way to start the new job. Creating HR nightmares right off the bat.

"It's such a pleasure to meet the rest of the family," she said, her neck heating up. She jerked her gaze away from the manly clan, sliding into the seat farthest away from Zahir. If she could just not look at him during the meeting, that would be great.

Even without looking at him, she could feel his gaze sizzling over her. The same way it had the night they met. So hot that it might char the edges of the table. Her neck heated up more—this was getting dangerous. It wasn't even hot in here.

"When Marian recommended you, we knew there was no other choice," Imaad said, tossing her a brilliant smile. Man, Marian had been right—these guys were *hot*. But she'd been wrong in one tiny aspect. Layla stole a glance at Zahir, feeling her insides crumple. Zahir was definitely the hottest. Hands down.

"I'm just grateful for the chance to be here." She tapped her fingers on the desk. Wasn't there something she could fan herself with?

"We looked over the resume you sent last night," Zahir started, his voice laced with professionalism. He rifled through some papers, his dark eyes darting over the sheets. "You have a very compelling early history in Human Resources. One that is rife with experience in conflict resolution and sensitive negotiations. And, I see, a penchant for travel."

"Oh, yes." She nodded vigorously, looking at each man except Zahir. "Travel is in my blood. I recently left the corporate world in New York to begin traveling but, uh," she licked at her lips, the imagine of Zahir hoisting her against her door flashing sinfully through her mind, "I could be willing to make Minarak my official destination for the next period of time."

"We should talk salary." Imaad shuffled some papers, glancing at his brothers. He ran through the job description, and she mentally ticked off each point as one of her areas of expertise. As if they'd designed the position just for her. "To be honest, we're keen to hire you. And we'll offer you the money to stay here for a while."

"Furnished apartment, relocation benefits, and a starting salary of one hundred thousand US dollars," Omar added.

Layla blinked, the words circling bulkily in her head. She'd made that much in New York City. But with almost zero spending required of her here in Minarak, the majority of that income could be banked. Marian had been right. A one-year trip could easily turn into two...or more. And better yet, she'd have options for afterward. That amount of money was worth postponing her trip by a little bit. A year would fly by.

Her stunned silence must have been enough of an answer.

"Shall we start with a year?" Almasi Senior rumbled with the suggestion, looking at everyone in turn. "Thirty days probation, though I doubt you'll need it."

Layla nodded, feeling like her head might topple right off. *Let's wrap it up so I can get out of here and start breathing again.* "Sounds great. I'm very eager to begin."

Zahir looked down at some papers in his hands. "Then we should sign."

Layla rolled her lips inward as she watched his perfect, masculine hands set aside her contract. Even the act of him clicking a pen was somehow sexy. She swallowed hard. She was in trouble. She'd already had a *taste* of this man. How was she supposed to ignore that delectable flavor from here on out?

He slid the contract her way, his dark gaze meeting hers for a scorching moment. "Have a look. Make sure everything seems fine. And then sign on the last page."

Layla nodded, feeling dazed. He could have told her to dance around the room with maracas, and she would have mutely agreed. She flipped through the pages, trying to make sense of the words, making it only a line or two before her nerves rattled and distracted her again.

Working here couldn't be like this all the time. She'd have her own office. Her own space. Her own ways of avoiding Zahir during work hours. She flipped to the last page, skimming the articles. She just needed to process the shock of walking into her big meeting to find her Parsian lover at the helm, and then she'd be fine.

Totally fine.

She signed the last page with a flourish, and satisfaction rippled through the room. Almasi Senior nodded while Imaad and Omar looked pleased. Zahir stared at some unknowable spot on the table, tapping a finger against the finish.

"Welcome to Almasi-Thomas," Omar said, grinning ear-to-ear.

Everyone shook hands again, and she made her handshake with Zahir as limp and efficient as possible. He was her boss now. They had to scrap everything that had come before, rewrite the entire rule book from scratch. And with her as the Human Resources Director of Cultural Integration, she actually *would* write the policies.

"Let me show you to your new office," Zahir blurted, stepping forward while his brothers shuffled toward the door. "Then you can start getting settled in."

Layla's stomach sank. Couldn't she request Omar show her the way? But no, this was just something she'd have to get used to—staring this sex god in the face and doing nothing.

"Great." She tried to sound cheery but it just came out strained. Maybe even a little crazed. Layla followed Zahir out of the board room and down the hallway. Toward the end, he pushed on the second-to-last door, revealing a spacious office with wooden floors. Empty bookshelves lined one wall. The windows overlooked downtown Minarak and, far in the distance, rolling dunes.

"Wow." She walked to the desk, already imagining ways she could fill this space, make it hers. But more than that, Zahir's presence crowded her mind, making it hard to think about nearly anything else. After a few tense seconds she heard the door click shut. She turned to see Zahir leaning against it, his gaze dark and heavy.

CHAPTER FIVE

"Well, this is a surprise."

His own words sounded foreign to him, resonating strangely in the empty office. Layla's expression was torn between indecision and something else he couldn't identify. She sank into the office chair.

"Yeah. You're telling me." She gnawed on her thumbnail, worried gaze studying something across the room. "I had no idea."

"Me, neither." He cleared his throat, stepping forward tentatively. Moving deeper into her space was dangerous. He wasn't sure if he could trust himself, not after wanting her so desperately all yesterday and this morning.

Her appearance in the board room had felt like the result of wanting her too hard, as if he'd thought her into existence but at the worst possible moment. After their incredible night of phone sex last night, he'd woken up with a hard-on and a rapidly unfolding plan for what they'd do that night. Dinner plans were in the works.

But now...

He stuffed his hands in his pockets, clenching his jaw. "What happened between us should stay there. Between us."

"Well, obviously." Layla huffed, pinching the bridge of her nose. "I'm not so excited about walking straight into the biggest HR shit show of my entire career."

"It won't be a shit show. I promise." He came up to her desk, his gaze traveling over as much of her as he could see. The arc of her neck. The creamy skin he'd caressed so many times the other night, was dying to caress again. He dragged a finger along the edge of her desk, thoughts roiling in his head. "I won't tell anyone what happened. And I assume it…won't happen again."

The words barely left his mouth. It seemed sacrilege to suggest, but how could it ever continue? The stakes were too high. Usually when Zahir had his trysts, he went full incognito. He'd *thought* that picking up a foreign woman was a safe bet— not that she'd be Marian's best friend and come waltzing into the office two days later for a position with his company.

Besides, if word got out that Zahir's lifestyle included picking up women at clubs and having as much sex as he did, his father would be furious. And the board members—all notoriously staunch conservatives—would lose their minds. Especially when it concerned the dutiful eldest son. He could already taste the backlash such an admission might inspire, and the mere thought made his stomach twist.

"Yeah. You got that right." Layla crossed her arms, shaking her head. But her gaze seemed to drift…maybe she was thinking about all the dirty things he'd whispered to her the night before. Or remembering the way she'd moaned into the phone as she came over and over again, just for him. A shudder traveled up his spine, chased by goosebumps. *Why couldn't you be anybody else?*

Her chest flushed, and the color crept into her neck. He palmed the smooth surface of her desk, desperate to say more, to take the conversation back to exactly where it shouldn't go. His office was *next door* to hers. Concentration might become impossible. Knowing that girlish squeals and trembling, fragrant orgasms lay just beyond the wall—if only they could find a way to do it in secret.

No. It can't continue. He needed to play that on repeat in his head.

"I want to help in any way I possibly can," he said, measuring his words. "Don't be afraid to come to me with questions or...anything." *Anything except sex or romance.*

"Who will I report to?"

He paused. "Me."

She laughed bitterly, shaking her head. "Why do I feel like I'm in some horrible rom-com movie right now?"

Zahir shoved his hands back in his pockets, finding himself desperate to get closer to her. He needed to exit, immediately. "I'll let you get settled in. Let me know if you need anything."

He left quickly, a dull headache sprouting. Would this be how life was from now on? Headaches because the most erotic and satisfying sexual encounters of his life came from the woman just out of his reach in his own building?

Now that their relationship had been unexpectedly thrust into quicksand, he needed to re-lay the foundation. Build up a formal, colleague-based trust. One that had nothing to do with the fact that his fingers, tongue, and dick had been buried inside of her within the past forty-eight hours.

He clenched his fists as he paced his office. Office fraternization was one thing. But if it got out that they'd been sleeping together before the job, there would be no limit to the blowback.

He'd start slow. He'd make pointed, platonic gestures.

And he'd do his best to avoid looking at her, thinking about her, or remembering anything about the magical two nights they'd shared. Because if he allowed himself to indulge in those memories, then he didn't have a shot in hell at keeping things business-only.

*   *   *

By the end of their first week as colleagues, Zahir couldn't label it a failure, but neither could he call it a success. It just *was*. A stilted, awkward, functional-pretenses charade at getting into a work groove. They came into contact far too often, and sometimes he wondered if some evil puppeteer was orchestrating their sudden encounters in the hallway or crossed lines on the phone. They even seemed to leave the office at the same time, despite Zahir trying to leave early or late to miss her.

The fact was he couldn't stay out of her way, even when he tried. And every night back at his penthouse, his fingers twitched with thoughts of sending another text, just to see where it might lead.

By the end of week two, he felt consumed with thoughts of Layla. In some ways, it grew easier: they had a certain kind of rapport, at least, and he could stop seeing tantalizing flashes of their time together when his mind wandered. They'd elbowed their way into a somewhat-normal conversational pattern, even bordered on joking around at times.

But he was dying for more of her, and that desire consumed him. Their short yet entertaining interactions begged for a deeper exploration. Even if they'd never met before her interview, he'd be entranced by her.

On Friday evening, a light rap sounded on his door. It was her—he knew because she had a delicate way of breaking his solitude, but also because the hairs of his arm stood on end. The unmistakable sign that Layla was nearby.

"Hey boss." She strolled into his office, holding folders in her hand. No doubt the drafts of the newest policies she'd been working on. "I have the information you requested."

He hated how she always reminded him of their professional standing at work, because it was the one thing he was desperate to forget. "Excellent. Any issues?"

He took the folders from her outstretched hand, sneaking a glance at her outfit for the day. A black blouse with a light gray skirt. Smart and simple, that was her style. But the roundness of her breasts and the curve of her hips made every smart and simple style too tempting to bear.

"None at all. I think I'm getting the hang of how things work around here. I've even mastered the email client."

"That deserves a celebration." He grinned up at her, a suggestion to grab drinks heavy on his tongue. But he stilled himself before he added it on. It would only reek of desperation.

"I hardly think so. Unless your bar is actually *that* low." She smirked.

He smiled. Sometimes, he could feel that energy pulsing between them. The energy that had been there from the second they locked eyes at Echo.

"Some employees require adjusting the bar," he replied.

She feigned offense. "I see where you're heading with that comment."

He laughed. "Isn't that part of the cultural sensitivity training you're developing?" He pressed his tongue into his cheek, loving the banter. He didn't joke with anyone else like this at work. Not even his brothers. "I'm just recognizing part of your American heritage."

Layla narrowed her eyes, but a laugh escaped her. "You jerk."

He shuffled papers on his desk, fighting a grin. Triumph pulsed through him; this was the type of interaction he wanted to cultivate more of. Because it seemed the only way he could get near her, to take her in.

"Any plans for the weekend?" He tried to sound offhand, even peered inside a desk drawer so he might seem non-committal.

"Oh, nothing major. Just my best friend's wedding…"

Her words slithered through him, and he sat up straight, dragging his gaze to meet hers. "That's right."

She cackled. "You forgot!"

"I didn't forget," he protested. *I was simply too caught up in trying to insert myself in your weekend path somehow.* But this was even better. He'd at least be *near* her. "I was just seeing if you remembered."

"Oh sure." She cocked a grin, strutting out of his office. "See you tomorrow, boss."

His gaze riveted on the sway of her hips as she left his office, his cock twitching in his pants. Two weeks in and this set-up was torture, pressure building every second. How would he last a year? Some pressure had to be let out or he'd explode.

Maybe the wedding would be the perfect place to let off a little pressure.

CHAPTER SIX

Layla arranged Marian's bouquet one last time as she perched on the edge of the clawfoot bathtub, waiting for Marian's makeup artist to finish. The ceremony would begin in a half hour, and Marian was the calmest bride she'd ever seen in her life.

"You like the veil?" Marian looked up at her, indecision flashing across her face. She'd opted for a vintage-style cream gown and pearl-dotted veil.

"I love it. And everything else." Layla took a sniff of the navy blue and soft pink blooms. "Your wedding is already the most epic affair I've ever attended."

"Why didn't you invite your Arabian stallion?" Marian squeezed her eyes shut as the makeup artist applied a setting spray to her face, and then blinked rapidly.

"Oh, he, uh...I don't know." Layla gnawed at the inside of her mouth. "I guess the stallion turned out to be more of a...pony." *Except he's still a stallion, and he's definitely here.*

Marian frowned. "Dang. I thought you'd already found your Mr. Parsabad."

Layla laughed, but it rang hollow and forced. "I'm sure there are plenty others."

"Maybe some at the reception, too!" Marian wiggled her perfectly plucked eyebrows and then swooped to standing. Her gown rustled as she reached for the bouquet. With one last look in the mirror, the ladies headed out into the fray, where plenty of Parsian and American women were finishing their own preparations.

Annabelle cooed when she saw Marian. "You look stunning."

After some phone pictures, it was time to go downstairs for the ceremony. Marian had opted for a laid-back fusion of the two cultures. Which meant that her wedding hung somewhere between traditional American and traditional Parsian. There'd be a bridal party and the first dances, which were common in both countries, but no garter or flower tossing, since that pushed the envelope for Parsabad.

What they wouldn't skimp on, Marian had told her, was the wine. It would flow like water from the mountaintops, and this part had Layla more excited than almost anything else. Because if there was one thing she liked about weddings, it was open bars and the chance to find a fun companion for the evening.

Even though she already knew exactly who she'd like her companion to be. The one man she shouldn't talk to, or even look at, once she was drunk.

Zahir.

His close proximity had her nerve endings on fire. Just knowing he was on the premises, dressed to kill, was enough to have her thighs quivering. Working side-by-side with Mr. Sex-On-Legs was hard enough. The informal situation might be the death of their platonic ruse.

Because Layla severely doubted she'd be able to keep the cork on if wine got involved.

Marian and Omar had rented out a centuries-old villa for their wedding and ensuing reception. The ceremony itself would happen outside on the sprawling lawn, where an imam waited beneath a golden arch near a sprawling backdrop of orchids and rose bushes. The air was fragrant and warm, and conversation drifted toward her as she neared to take her place in the processional. She and Annabelle were the bridesmaids, and Marian's father would walk her down the aisle.

Which meant of course Zahir would be at her side down the aisle.

He gave her a cheeky grin as she approached, his gaze traveling wantonly up and down her body.

"You look lovely," he said quietly, offering his arm. The conversation of the seated audience dulled to a roar, and a string quartet played near the imam.

"Thank you," she responded, feeling her cheeks heat up as she slid her arm through his. "So do you."

And he did. The man's suit probably cost thousands of dollars, and nobody could fill it out as well as he did.

He cinched her close to him, his cologne clouding her senses. Something had to be wrong with her, that she couldn't get over their hookup. He just…he was too good. She needed just a little bit more.

They took their place in line as the music waxed, behind Annabelle and Imaad. Omar stood at the arch, grinning from ear to ear, no doubt awaiting that first glimpse of Marian.

"Just know I'm not flattering you," Zahir whispered, leaning down. "You look so sexy I don't know that I'll be able to walk straight down this aisle."

Her breath caught in her throat, and her gaze snapped up to meet his. His dark eyes swirled with mischief.

"I thought we said—"

"We're not at work, and it's a fact." He smiled smugly.

"You're bending the rules."

"Perhaps." They took a few steps forward, the music signaling their cue. "But I certainly haven't broken them."

*   *   *

Hours later, Layla nursed her third glass of wine, her mind still making circles around Zahir's words. The ceremony had been lovely, pictures fun and efficient, and now the reception was moving along without a hitch.

Everyone was shiny-faced and happy, the villa roaring with conversation and laughter. Layla needed a time-out. She'd reached that part of the equation—extroversion plus social niceties multiplied by cake and wine—where she needed to wander to a quiet spot, get some fresh air, remind herself who she was in this whole mix.

She slipped away from her table, where Annabelle and Imaad had been conversing with old friends of the family. She wandered down a carpeted hallway, the music and conversation fading slightly. Dragging her fingers along the floral wallpaper, she headed toward the kitchen and then down a different hallway.

After a few turns, the chatter of the party was no longer evident. A breeze reached her from somewhere, and she turned one last corner. At the end of the darkened hallway, someone stood looking out an open bay window. Layla started to turn, until she realized who it was.

Of course it's him.

She froze in her spot, unable to decide if she should disappear or make herself known. He seemed to be having a private moment, much like her. She'd be intruding. Horribly.

"Layla."

His smooth voice soothed her rattled nerves, and she deflated a bit. She moved toward him as though by instinct.

"Why are we always running into each other?" His words were pensive. He watched as she walked toward him, his hands buried in his pockets.

"Seems we just can't help it." She rolled her lips inward, gaze skating over the view from the window. Rolling lawn, manicured bursts of flowers, statues lining the paved walkway.

"Or maybe you *wanted* to find me."

She swallowed hard. "Trust me, that wasn't my intent." She swept her hand back toward where she'd come from. "I don't even know how I got here. I just needed to take a minute."

Zahir leaned against the wall, his gaze raking over her. "Hopefully you'll stay longer than a minute."

She laughed nervously. Testosterone rolled off him in waves. Memories flooded her of their night together. Her pussy clenched in response.

"You're blushing," Zahir said a moment later. "What are you thinking about?"

She squeezed her eyes shut. *Stop betraying me, fair skin.* "Nothing. I just...blush."

"Hmmm." He shifted closer, his spicy cologne reaching her. "I think I know what you were thinking about."

Oh god. Here we go. They were diving head first back into the fire, and she was powerless to stop it. "Oh yeah?"

"You were thinking about us."

She huffed with a laugh, trying to feign something easygoing. "Please. Don't be so full of yourself."

"Was I wrong?"

She opened her mouth to shut him down, but his sexy grin distracted her.

"Exactly." He stepped closer, his voice lowering a notch. "I know—I suffer the same. I think about you all the time."

Her eyes fluttered shut. What delicious torture this was. She wanted to surrender. "Do you?"

"Mm-hmm." He sidled behind her, his breath hot on her ear. "Sometimes, I want you so bad I have to do the job myself."

She inhaled sharply as his hand slid over the dip of her waist. She stiffened, desperate for more. He nipped at her earlobe, shivers chasing goose bumps up and down her arms.

"God." She gripped the wooden ledge of the windowsill, suddenly unsteady. He hooked her around the waist, bringing her solidly against the sturdy frame of his body.

"I can tell you more…if you want to hear it." His lips brushed her ear, and she made a noise, something she hadn't even permitted to escape her lips. Desire stormed her, staining her panties, making her weak.

"Tell me," she whispered, keeping her eyes shut. As if maybe that would make it okay. Less of a breach of propriety and more of a fantasy that hadn't happened.

"Sometimes I have to touch myself right there in my office," he growled, rocking his hips against her. The hard ridge of his cock jutted against her lower back. "Especially when you wear those gray pants that show off every last curve of your ass."

She gulped. This was like bringing their sexy phone talk to life, and it was a million times hotter this way.

"I always picture you in my head," he whispered. "One time you almost caught me."

"Mmm." She rubbed her ass in a slow circle against him, pressing her head against his neck. "More. Tell me more."

"I think about bending you over my desk and pushing up your black skirt all the way to your waist. And then I'll take a big bite of each ass cheek before I press myself between your legs, all the way until there's nothing left to bury."

She gave a shuddery moan. "Jesus, Zahir. Is this still bending the rules?"

He chuckled low, suckling at her neck. "No, I broke them."

His words seared through her like a lightning bolt. They'd broken the rules—there was no putting this rule back together. For today, at least. They could resume the pact next week.

"Listen." Clarity struck her like a slap on the face, and she spun to face him. She grabbed his face in her hands, his barely-there scruff tugging at the sensitive pads of her fingers. "We break the rules today, but only today. Got it?"

He nodded, his eyes glinting black, as if he himself was the precipice to the dark side. Oh, how she wanted to go over him.

"Clearly there's some…pressure, here. And we should release it." She tugged his shirt out from his pants and slid a hand up to meet the warm skin of his belly. She sighed—he was rock solid under there, pure lines and abs. "Fuck. Why do you feel so good?"

He smiled lazily. "I could ask you the same."

"But after today, we're back to the agreement. This is a…one off. One sanctioned slip. *Okay?*"

Zahir nodded, and then Layla pressed her lips to his so hard they tingled. Needy kisses erupted, turning sloppy and then lewd, kisses that rooted her to her spot and made her mind's eyes turn blinding white. Zahir held her against the windowsill, his cock pressed to low belly, and then his strong hands swept beneath her, hoisting her up to sit on the ledge.

She gasped through a kiss and then rocked back and forth to hoist her dress up to her waist so her legs could wrap around him, never breaking the seal. He smiled as he smoothed a hand up her thigh, the touch of him sending a wave of heat rippling through her.

"I missed you," he murmured.

"We see each other every day," she said between kisses, but she knew what he meant. She missed him in a way that didn't make sense. Their working relationship was only a fraction of what she craved from him.

"It's not the same." He ground his pelvis against her, and then reached down to open his fly. A moment later he fished his cock out of his briefs, giving it a long pull. Then he rummaged in his coat pocket, revealing his wallet. He was going for the condom.

Layla ran her hand over the silky skin of his cock, desperate to feel him inside her again. The clock was ticking. This was an outlandish and inappropriate thing, to fuck in the hallway of a villa during Marian's wedding. But they had to. Their passion demanded it.

A moment later he rolled the condom on, and then Zahir nudged himself between her legs, the swollen head of his cock pressing past her panties into the slick cleft of her pussy. She gasped and hooked her arms around his neck, never breaking his gaze as he eased himself into her, so slowly that she had to bite back a groan.

"Layla." The breathiness in his voice told him exactly what she needed to know—that this sensation was off the charts for both of them, not just her. He slid into her with intolerable slowness, her pussy pulsing and clenching around him. He let out a guttural noise as he buried himself deeper. She arched toward him, starbursts blooming behind her eyelids. She wanted this all the time. She wanted *him* all the time.

A string of words in Farsi tumbled from his lips, and then he started pumping. She hooked her ankles behind his back, knotting a hand in the lapels of his coat, her body already tense and ready to pop.

"I'm close," he said, his voice ragged.

"Me too." She swallowed a moan as he rolled against the taut nub of her clit. She pressed her forehead into his chest, breaths escalating as the tension climbed.

He rocked into her again and again, each time bringing her lightyears closer to orgasm. On the third thrust, she fell over the edge, pleasure rocketing through her limbs so fast that she went limp in his arms.

The sticky sweet waves of her orgasm subsided as he stilled against her, groaning into her neck. Once his breathing calmed, she tilted her head up to look at him, finding the same buzzing happiness in his expression.

He smoothed his lips against hers, back and forth, and for a long time, neither broke the embrace.

CHAPTER SEVEN

On Monday morning, Zahir felt like he was in a lust hangover.

One full day of rest and lounging hadn't cleared his head after the wedding. He and Layla hadn't talked on Sunday, despite the fact that they spent the rest of the reception parked at the table, sipping wine and chatting like old friends. It left him dying to text her, touch base, just hear her voice the next day. But he abstained, because what they did had been wrong, and it couldn't—wouldn't—happen again.

Disbelief made circles in his mind, alongside relief. On the one hand, how had he been so stupid? If they'd gotten caught—by *anyone*—it could have been the biggest scandal of the year. Especially if any of the board members had caught wind. On the other hand, it was exactly what he'd craved, what he *needed*. Too much longer without giving into that passion and he might have snapped.

Layla breezed into the office looking completely normal. Sexy as always, her strawberry-gold hair swept back into a loose bun. Affectionately disinterested.

"Morning, Zahir." She popped her head into his office as normal, to let him know she was there.

"Morning." He flicked a pen against his fingertips, wanting to say more. "Did you have a good weekend?"

Her distant smile turned icy. "Why, yes, I did. How about you?"

"Oh, yes. Extremely satisfying."

She nodded, then spun on her heels and strutted past his office. Zahir rubbed at his face. How was this stuff supposed to work? Playing it normal would never be possible. Not with this elephant in the room.

A moment later Layla strode into his office, shutting the door behind her. She came up to his desk looking like she might pull a gun out of her cleavage.

"Okay, listen. You know exactly what we did this weekend. So why even ask?"

He let a breath of air he'd been holding. "I was just trying to be casual. Normal. You know, like I thought you wanted."

She groaned with frustration. "This is why these things never work. We made a mistake. It can't happen again. *Can. Not.*"

Disappointment crashed through him. "Got it."

"What happened on Saturday was a one-time mistake. We were getting to casual and normal, but this weekend ruined it. And you just happened to catch me at a vulnerable moment with some really convincing sexy talk which, additionally, is a comment that will be forgotten as soon as I leave this office."

A laugh escaped him despite his better judgment. "Right. Understood."

"And we won't talk about Saturday, or this conversation, again." Her nostrils flared as she appraised him a final time, and then she spun on her heels and stormed out of the office.

So that made her stance clear. He crumpled into his seat. Her words had deflated him, left him feeling not just put in his place but also...disappointed. Like the tiny flame of hope inside him had been whooshed out of existence.

But hope for what? He straightened his back, busying himself in his emails. Somewhere deep inside, there'd been a hope for something with Layla. Not that it made sense or that he even had any idea what that something meant.

But there was something about her that demanded attention, an essence or energy that captivated as much as it left him wanting more.

Distraction would be key from here on out. He needed to put on his game face and stick to the plan. Because being around her five days a week without the power to prod, delve, or touch was a special type of challenge, one that he'd need all his reserves to overcome.

*   *   *

Layla flopped onto her couch with a satisfied groan. Four weeks. Four weeks at the new job under her belt, and once again she and Zahir were on their way to being regular, normal, non-sexually-active coworkers.

She flipped onto her back, studying the dappled ceiling of her new apartment. It was a three-bedroom with a balcony in the heart of Minarak, not that she needed three bedrooms. But her pay package included it, and it was sorta luxurious, and now whenever she had guests she could offer them their own room instead of a lame blow-up mattress next to her own bed.

One month at the job. Two weeks in her new apartment. One week, six days, and two hours since Zahir had last penetrated her. She groaned, tugging at her hair. She had to stop *thinking* things like that. But they sprouted unbidden inside of her, like a clingy weed she had to keep uprooting and spraying with dangerous chemicals.

But yet it persisted. The sinuous thoughts, wending their way through her mind.

At least it was better at work. Ever since his stern talking-to, Zahir had behaved himself like a choir boy. He barely even looked at her, which relieved as much as it infuriated. And most days, it felt like they were simply playing a game, one in which the rules were crystal clear until they weren't.

63

Because she didn't trust herself to not fall back into his arms sometime over the next year. And she didn't trust him to not let it happen. Especially if anything brought them together over a free weekend.

She needed to find a new dude and stat. Not that she advocated for distraction via the male gaze, but Zahir was a tough one to forget. Uprooting him simply wasn't enough. She had to replace him so that new roots could take over.

Yeah. That seemed like it made the most sense. She rolled off the couch, eager to snack on the hummus she'd found at a neighborhood market. It looked homemade and ultra-tasty. She hadn't had much of an appetite for breakfast the past few days, which left her starving by lunchtime and super ready for snacks after work. After that, she'd open some wine and settle into her favorite Friday routine—getting ready to go out.

Marian and Omar were still on their honeymoon. They'd planned for a long getaway, and by her calculations, they were probably somewhere in Iceland by now. Things at work had been busier for Zahir in Omar's absence, which was a blessing. Anything to lessen the chances of them running into each other.

Four weeks down. Only forty-eight to go. She sighed as she rummaged through the fridge, pulling out the hummus and a bag of carrots. It wasn't like she was counting down or anything. She sorta liked having the stable job in a foreign country. It was a cool way to explore a new country while living there. She hadn't done much proper exploration yet, but it would come in time.

Most of the exploration you've done has been Zahir's body.

The thought slammed through her and she almost dropped the carrots. Dammit. If only she could stop those thoughts, her life would be so much easier. She'd get around to traveling Parsabad. It wouldn't *only* be Zahir's body soon enough. Maybe she'd take a day trip tomorrow. Somewhere cool and new.

Yeah. That sounded good. She plopped the carrots and hummus onto her coffee table and reached for her laptop. A quick search would help her find exactly what she was looking for. Fun, affordable, and perfect for single ladies.

Once her laptop was on, she reached for a carrot, swirling it in the hummus. She crunched into it as her operating system flashed to life. She moaned in approval when the hummus hit her taste buds. Definitely homemade.

Does Zahir make hummus? The thought stepped tentatively through her brain space. She should find out. She swirled the bitten end of her carrot into the hummus again, crunching a second time. Except no—she wouldn't ask him. Because that would be getting personal. And that wasn't *allowed.*

She sighed. Better to just plan a little getaway and get over the Zahir complex. With enough time, this plan had to work—the *avoid-and-forget* approach.

She typed in a Google search and scrolled through results, ideas sparking to life. Some of these destinations would be awesome for long weekends. Spa environments, hiking trails, even camel rides through the desert. *Didn't Annabelle do something like that?* She vaguely recalled a story about Imaad wooing her in a Bedouin tent. *Maybe Zahir and I could...*

No. Wrong thought. She doubled down on her efforts to concentrate, clicking through the options for a day trip from Minarak. She'd have to rent a car or even hire a taxi, but that would be easy enough. Maybe she could get a recommendation through the Almasis. That would be a totally legitimate reason to call Zahir over the weekend.

She pinched her eyes shut. It just wouldn't stop, would it? She crunched into another carrot. Her sex drive had been ravenous the past few days. She was getting off every night at bedtime and then again in the morning sometimes too. Maybe it was her time of the month—she always seemed to get a little more amped up around then. That would explain the Zahir thoughts, at least.

That or the fact that he's drop dead sexy and the best lay of your life.

She groaned as she opened the computer calendar. When *was* her last period? She certainly hadn't bled since her first hook up with Zahir. And the first time was…a month ago. She struggled to think when her last period fell, swallowing a big chunk of carrot that made her cough. She could have sworn it was a week or so before leaving New York. Because she'd been over it by the time she had her going away party, which had been…

She consulted the calendar again, furrowing a brow. *Wow.* It had been *way* over a month since her last period, and that was maybe still being conservative. She reached for another carrot, nibbling it while her brain worked through the math. Why would she be late? She was never late. She didn't use birth control, but she also didn't have unprotected sex.

You can't be pregnant. The thought soothed her, made it seem like a fact. She and Zahir had used a condom both times. She'd seen him use it herself. Heard him rip open the package. She was safe and protected.

She swallowed hard, thinking back over the past week. Each morning she'd felt a little off, but was it maybe, somehow, a sign? Not necessarily a pregnancy sign, but just a totally-normal-late-period sign.

Her hand hovered over another carrot as a sneaky thought crept through her head. *What if you've been starting to have morning sickness?*

She hadn't eaten breakfast for the past three days. Just hadn't wanted to. That didn't mean she was *pregnant* though.

She tried to laugh it off, as if it might convince the reality of the situation to join in on her reasoning. This was just a blip. A late period due to moving. A random bout of nausea because she was acclimating to a new diet, a new eating lifestyle.

She blinked a few times, trying to go back to planning her day trip. But the thought hung threatening and bulky in the back of her mind. A distant threat. It pushed her to her feet and out the door.

It was simple. She'd buy a test and find out, once and for all. It wouldn't be dramatic or hard, it was simply the easiest way to resolve this niggling worry. Besides, she couldn't take a day trip while she wondered.

She certainly couldn't enjoy that bottle of wine if she wondered, either.

It's fine. Your body is just adjusting. Remember that time you went to England and your period disappeared for two months afterward? She reassured herself on her way to the corner store, which also had a small pharmacy inside. A blast of cool, dry air met her as she pushed into the store. She browsed each aisle until she found what she was looking for, the telltale rectangular box with a picture on the front showing a positive test result. She paid quickly and hurried back to her apartment, heart knocking against her ribs.

Your body is just adjusting. She repeated it like a mantra. She couldn't be pregnant. She *wouldn't* be pregnant. Because that wasn't in her plans, and it was very likely never to be in her future.

Settling down and having someone's baby—that had never been part of her life plan. Not since she'd realized at age sixteen that she could go anywhere, be anyone, do literally anything she wanted and to hell with anyone who told her otherwise. Her family's urgings to settle down and start a family only pushed her in the opposite direction. She was the girl who quit the corporate life to go gallivanting around the world during her prime childbearing years. *Even though sometimes you get stuck in another corporate job immediately after.*

She ripped open the packaging, fumbling to find the English section of the instructions sheet. Maybe it wasn't stress or long-distance moves; maybe she had cysts or something. That could be it. Her finger trembled as she underlined the English directions. This might just be cysts after all.

The sheet told her to wait until morning for the best results, but she didn't have time. Tomorrow morning, she'd either be day-tripping or crying into her pillow. It had to be *now.*

She stumbled toward the bathroom on Jello knees and perched over the stick, grunting as she tried to force a pee. Finally a trickle emerged, and she aimed it just right. She doused the stick, and then she waited.

Layla didn't even get up from the toilet as she waited for the stick to tell her her fate. She clutched at her hair, heart hammering in her throat, counting seconds so she didn't peek too soon and see a wrong result.

When an eternity of seconds had crept by, she finally allowed herself the answer. She snatched up the stick, her belly tight with tension as she looked at the small window.

Two lines.

She blinked a few times, letting the news wash over her. A strange cocktail of emotions burbled through her, but she couldn't make sense of that now.

The test clattered to the floor and she yanked her pants up, running to her phone. She needed Marian, wherever she was. And she just prayed to God she picked up.

CHAPTER EIGHT

Zahir's gut felt tense as he locked up his office prior to the weekend. He'd stayed late to finish up a few pending reports for Omar during his absence. Of course Omar had taken the longest honeymoon known to mankind, but Zahir could hardly blame him. Their travel route was admirable and even something of his own fantasy. Hell, getting out of the country more often was becoming more and more of a scandalous thought. Almost as scandalous as his constant thoughts of Layla.

His gut wrenched again. It was like he couldn't help but link everything back to her, so much that he wondered if he needed to call her. Maybe she was in trouble somewhere, and this was her signal for help.

Are you crazy? Two full weeks of minimal contact hadn't lessened his urges or attraction any more than it had before; it simply made it necessary to distract himself. Which, thankfully, came in the form of work. And masturbation. *Lots* of masturbation.

A familiar gruff voice interrupted his quiet walk down the hallway. His father curled a finger in the air, beckoning for him to follow. Zahir altered his path to go to his father's office.

"I'm surprised you're here this late," Zahir said, closing the door behind him.

"I just got off the phone with an important person." His father's eyes twinkled as he sat behind his desk. "I would have called you if I hadn't found you leaving the office. I have some news for you."

There was a note of joviality in his father's voice, one that Zahir wasn't accustomed to hearing. This was either a huge business deal or...he couldn't even guess what might make his father this giddy. "Do tell."

"Zahir, my son, I think it's time that we begin to prepare for you to assume control here."

The words floated heavily in the air, like a tanker in the ocean. Zahir tapped out a slow rhythm on the arm rest of his chair, struggling to fully process the words.

"I'm flattered." Of course, he'd known this day would come. He just hadn't expected it so soon.

"You're flattered, and you're readier than ever. We've been preparing you for this day. I have full confidence that everything will go smoothly, but we should begin the transition immediately." His father paused, clearing his throat, ensuring perfect delivery. "And part of that preparation includes your getting married."

Every bone and cell inside Zahir's body froze. He reluctantly met his father's stern gaze. "Ah." *Married. Fuck.* He'd avoided it long enough. As a bachelor thirty-three-year-old, he was practically a unicorn in his country. With his two younger brothers already married, sometimes it felt a little embarrassing. Not that he minded continuing his bachelor life in any way.

"I've arranged a bride for you." A grin flickered on his father's face. "She's a beautiful girl, very smart, unspoiled—" That was code for *virgin*. "Absolutely perfect for you. And this arrangement will greatly satisfy some of our board members."

Zahir's gaze swept over the desktop, focusing on the dark stain of the wood. There were so many elaborate swirls there. Far too many to even count. And suddenly, he was far more interested in counting the swirls than continuing this conversation. "I—I'm not sure what to say."

"Say you're ready to set a date." His father leaned forward a bit. "If we hurry, it could be before the end of the year."

Zahir blinked, something jerking inside his chest. "I'm in no mood to get married right now."

His father grumbled a bit, some of that glow falling off his face. "Mood? Who needs to be in a mood to get married? This is a business arrangement. You're the one we planned to take over for me, but the board will only support it if you're married."

Zahir swallowed hard, his tongue sticking to the roof of his mouth. The mention of the board could silence him even as his father's news stabbed him in the heart. "I understand that."

"Then there's nothing further to discuss. I trust you'll make the right decision." His father grumbled again, and then added, "That's all. Enjoy your weekend, son."

Zahir stood on unsteady legs, drifting more than walking back toward the hallway. All the way out of the office, sullen thoughts crowded his mind. *Goodbye bachelor life. Hello shackles and boredom.* He turned toward the elevators, pushing the down button. *Can't I just marry Layla instead?*

He rubbed at his face inside the elevator, as if it might help wipe away some of the confusion. He'd gone from bachelor to betrothed in the span of five minutes, so he needed to get used to the idea. Find a good bottle of whisky. And do his best not to sulk and pine and spend every second of his weekend wondering what Layla was doing.

Because that had been his gut reaction—the surprise engagement felt like a betrayal to Layla. Of course that was absurd—they had no formal relationship to speak of. But there was only one person every fiber of his being craved, like a sun-parched wanderer seeking water. *Layla.*

What could he do now? The timeline of a pending marriage prompted desperation to flood his veins, as if he had to scoop up every last available moment with her before time ran out. Before she changed her mind, before the passion ran dry, before his business marriage took place. Any number of things waited to squash this passion that consumed him on a daily basis.

Need burbled through him, a familiar sensation taking an even-more-familiar path when it came to Layla. He knew what the right choice was, even if it was also technically the wrong choice.

He had no time to waste. He'd make sure Layla knew he intended to break the rules over and over again, for as long as he could get away with it. There was no other option besides Layla.

CHAPTER NINE

Layla came into work on Monday feeling simultaneously drained and refreshed. Her day-trip to a nearby city and antiquities museum had been a pleasant distraction from the shit show of her family planning, which had always been very simple: don't start a family. She'd cried enough tears in her apartment to fill a small lake. The shock and confusion had ebbed into a babbling brook of quiet despair.

She was going to be a mother, the only thing she'd never envisioned for herself.

The weekend featured all the stages of grief—denial, outrage, and eventual acceptance. Marian counseled her as well as she could from across the world as she and Omar packed their bags to come home from their honeymoon. She murmured sweet, helpful things while Layla cried. She hadn't even judged her when she admitted that Zahir was the father of her baby. Marian didn't seem surprised, or maybe she'd just expertly squashed her incredulity. Either way, she swore her friend to secrecy.

Because there was one thing she was certain of: Zahir wouldn't know.

Here begins the circus side show. She strolled into the hallway, dreading peeking into Zahir's office to say good morning. But she had to do it—normalcy was the goal. Along with platonic gestures and never fantasizing about her boss ever again. Especially while she carried his tiny collection of cells inside her belly.

The fucking condom broke. The thought burst through her head like fireworks with startling regularity, interrupting mundane tasks like brushing her teeth or heating up food in the microwave. It just didn't seem fair. There were mothers all over the world who wanted kids and couldn't have them. And here she was, careful enough to be protected, never wanting a child, and she gets the unlucky broken condom.

"Good morning." She forced a quick grin as she poked her head into Zahir's office. He was studying his computer as he was most mornings. His face lit up when he saw her.

"Morning." He offered a knee-buckling smile, his mouth hanging open like he might add more. She rushed away before she had to look at him any longer.

Inside the quiet of her own office, she took a long, deep breath, trying to roll some of the tension out of her shoulders. *Just get through the day.* It had to be easier going forward. And once she started to show, she could start working from home. She had plenty of time to begin that transition to remote work. There would be a way to make it work.

Zahir can't know.

As she settled into place behind her desk, thoughts roiled thick and chunky inside her head. She'd combed through every possible scenario of how this might turn out, since seeing the positive result. And the one thing that didn't make sense to her was telling Zahir.

He probably wanted to be a father, maybe someday, with the right wife cherry-picked for him by his family. The way Annabelle had been chosen for Imaad, the way Omar had married his first wife. After seeing all the traditional aspects of Omar and Marian's wedding, there was no doubt in Layla's mind that a surprise baby out of wedlock would not be well received by the Almasi clan. In fact, it might even ruin Zahir's professional life.

All of Marian and Annabelle's stories about Parsian culture and traditions haunted Layla every time she considered what it might be like to tell Zahir she was pregnant. She remembered the way Zahir had slipped out of her room that first night by a certain hour, to avoid the speculation. Well, now there was no speculating. He'd knocked someone up.

Confusion lashed at her, pushing her face into her hands. A quiet rap on her door made her bolt upright.

"Who is it?" She fumbled around at her desk, trying to make it look like she'd been working instead of moping.

"Zahir." The doorknob turned and he pushed the door open, poking his head in. "May I?"

78

She nodded, clearing her throat. "Sure. What's up?" She folded her fingers together on the desk top, made sure her midsection was firmly hidden behind the desk. Not like he could tell she was pregnant already. She couldn't be more than five weeks along. But still. Just in case.

"Just wanted to see how your weekend was." He leaned against the doorframe, impossibly casual and warm.

"Great." She shrugged. *Cried myself to sleep because I'm carrying your unexpected baby, is all.* "I checked out the antiquities museum in Shahaar. Spent some time in the desert. It was nice."

"Oh?" He lifted a brow. "Shahaar is one of my favorite places. I wish you had let me know. I could have taken you."

She swallowed a bitter laugh. "Well, that would hardly be appropriate for a working relationship, Zahir. I see you at the office, and that's it."

He tutted, an uncomfortable pause emerging. "Right. Well, I actually wanted to mention something that takes you out of the office."

Anxiety slithered through her. She had no energy left to confront this man. "What's that?"

"There's a dinner tonight." He slid his hands into his pockets, looking rather pleased with himself. "Business dinner, rather.

Strategy, check-ins, that sort of thing. Omar and Marian should be there, now that they're back from their eternal honeymoon."

Layla grinned but squashed it immediately. "Is it required?"

"Well, no…" Zahir's gaze fell to the floor. "But it would be beneficial for you to attend. A good way to touch base with colleagues. Plus, the food is great."

Work dinner wouldn't be so bad. And with Marian there, she'd have reinforcements if needed. There was no good reason to say no—other than the fact that looking at Zahir's face made her insides hurt. "Sure. Just let me know when and where."

"Great." Zahir smiled again, his gaze lingering on her face. The same warmth passed between them that had ensnared her the moment they started talking at Echo.

She forced a tight smile, ripping her gaze from his impeccably handsome jawline. "Okay then. See you later."

Layla gritted her teeth as Zahir took the hint and excused himself, whooshing out a deep breath once her door clicked shut. This was hell. No, actually it was worse than hell.

Not only was she pregnant out of wedlock in the most traditional country she'd ever set foot in, the pregnancy brought up all sorts of questions she wasn't ready to face. Did she even want it? Now that she was pregnant, having the baby seemed the only way. Considering the alternative just didn't sit right with her. But doing this on her own? It would be one thing if she'd been in a committed relationship and they had an accident. But even that was unlikely. Layla didn't let herself get into committed relationships. She liked to be the fun time, a fleeting comet of perfect conversation and amazing sex that never once fizzled into flagging attraction or awkward disappointments.

It was much easier that way.

Because that way, she never had to confront anything unsavory. No heartbreak, no letdowns, nothing other than strictly what she wanted. Why be in a relationship when she could be free? It had been her motto since finding out the hard way that getting rejected hurt big-time, and there was no way to prevent the other person from just deciding one day he no longer loved her.

It had happened right after college, when her boyfriend of six years just abandoned their apartment one day and never returned. She'd found out later he'd skipped town to go marry someone he'd met on a free dating service, a relationship that had fermented quietly right under her nose for at least a year. She'd thought she'd get the happily ever after, but instead she'd gotten burned.

No one else would get the chance to hurt her again. And if anything, throwing a baby into the mix only widened the doorway of vulnerability. If she told Zahir, he could shut them out or worse, make her a prisoner to his demands. No, it was better to handle this on her own. She'd be a single mother. Women did it every day, all around the world.

Once she banked a few more paychecks, she'd figure out where to deliver, and how to get out of her contract. Step by step. Things would come together.

She took a shaky breath, struggling to feel a sense of calm about it all, until a hiccup emerged and gut-wrenching sobs wracked her body.

CHAPTER TEN

Zahir twirled the stem of his wine glass back and forth under his fingers, allowing himself just one more glance at Layla. He knew he'd been staring at her throughout dinner, but it was impossible to look away. She'd shown up to work distant and distracted, which made him even more desperate to catch her eye and know that she was okay. Layla had a strange way of wearing her emotions on her sleeve. Or maybe he was simply the only one who could see them.

"I'd say we've done a fine job of mixing cultures and blending practices," Imaad spoke up, breaking through Zahir's thoughts. Imaad raised his wine glass, the rest of the table following suit. The group, which included all levels of executives, had been discussing overall business strategies, along with the benefits and challenges of the merger. Zahir was quick to point out Layla's contributions when he could, though he swore she shrank a little each time he did.

The table dissolved into individual conversations, and Zahir took another sip of his wine as Layla stood, gesturing discreetly to Marian. The two hurried away, leaving Layla's spot empty directly in front of him. Omar leaned toward him, gripping the back of his chair.

"Okay. Let me be plain." He cleared his throat, his dark eyes darting over Zahir's face. "Do you have a thing for your new hire?"

Zahir blinked a few times, struggling to find words. Was it so obvious?

"Or maybe you're already sleeping together." Omar lifted a brow.

"What are you talking about?" Zahir finally found his voice, and it came out more defensive than he liked.

"I know you. You have one thing written on your face."

Zahir tugged at the collar of his shirt. There was something unnerving about being called out, even if it was by his brother. He'd thought this attraction was far more under wraps. "And what's that?"

"You're looking to fuck."

Zahir's laugh came out sharp and forced. "Please. This is just how I look normally. I can't control it." He shifted in his seat, dragging his thumb over the base of his wine glass. "Besides. It doesn't matter what I want. I'm an engaged man now."

Omar sat back in his seat, crossing his arms. "You gave father your answer?"

"No, I haven't." He sighed. "But does it matter? It's as good as done."

"You could say no."

Zahir shook his head. "I can't. I could never. You know this better than anyone."

"You've sacrificed enough for the job, for the family. I'm sure you could—" Omar began.

"No." Zahir straightened in his seat, the mere suggestion making his blood run hot. "Not after everything father has done for me. I owe him everything. It's my obligation as the eldest. You don't understand."

Omar narrowed his eyes. "Father puts pressure on Immad and me too, you know. And I've managed to say no before."

"That was different." Of course Omar would bring up how he'd turned down arranged marriage offers after his first wife's death.

Omar eyed him for a moment and then focused on something toward the back of the room. Zahir spotted Marian and Layla wending their way through the restaurant toward them, heads close as they spoke.

"I trust your honeymoon went well." Zahir tapped his fingers on the tablecloth, unable to rip his gaze from Layla. It didn't matter whom he married or how hard he tried to be happy in the arranged marriage—he would never forget Layla. He'd never be able to not *see* her.

"Better than well." Omar flashed a mysterious grin, tipping the last of his wine into his mouth. "Marian and I are trying for a baby."

Zahir's brows shot up. It shouldn't surprise him, he just hadn't expected that he could be an uncle anytime soon. "Is that right? Congrats, brother. That's excellent."

"We'll see how long it takes. But I think I can safely say we'll be the first." Omar nudged him as he stood up. Zahir downed the rest of his wine, trying to spot where Layla had wandered off to. Marian approached the table alone.

"I'm certainly going to be in last place," Zahir said, coming to his feet. He buttoned his suit, furtively searching the restaurant for Layla as Marian slid into Omar's embrace. "But only in this instance."

Omar huffed with a laugh, and Marian smiled sweetly up at him. "What are you two talking about?"

"Just how he's definitely going to be an uncle before he's a father," Omar said, pushing his fingers into Marian's curls. Her smile wavered and then tightened.

"Well, let's get going." She jerked her head toward the door. "See you tomorrow, Zahir. Bright and early."

"Don't forget. You're back from vacation now." Zahir watched as the two strolled off to say goodbye to their colleagues, and then he surveyed the remaining crowd. Urgency clawed at him; he had to find Layla. Now might be his only chance to speak with her outside of a work setting, this slim window between responsibility and free time.

Instead of saying goodbye to anyone, Zahir hurried toward the front doors of the restaurant. He suspected she'd sneaked out early, after Marian came back alone. Maybe she was already gone. He pushed through the front doors of the restaurant, the rush of traffic and the dry, night air meeting him. At the curb, peering down the street, that familiar strawberry blonde hair tugged at his attention, the perfectly plaited tresses drawing him near.

"Layla." He jogged toward her and she turned, her face wrought into an unknown expression. She didn't hold his gaze long before turning back toward the street.

"What?" She held up her arm, gesturing more forcefully for a taxi.

He stood at her side, unsure what to say. Her icy exterior was palpable, but he wasn't sure how to melt it. "Are you leaving so soon?"

"The dinner is over. I'm ready for bed." She didn't even turn his way to speak.

Zahir reached for her wrist, gently guiding her hand down. "I can take you home."

She shook her head. "I don't think that's a good idea."

"Why? Because spending money for a stranger to take you somewhere is a better idea?" He scoffed, fishing out his phone before she could protest. "It's no trouble to drop you off."

Her gaze landed on his hands as he texted his driver to meet them out front. "You really shouldn't."

Zahir sent his text before slipping the phone back into his pocket. "Well, I already did." He smiled at her, as if encouraging her to do the same. She stared past him, her face neutral.

"Everything okay?"

She nodded, glancing at him briefly. "Yeah. It's been a long day. I'm tired." She folded her arms over her chest, turning away toward the street. A tense silence settled in the space between them on the sidewalk, one that Zahir couldn't figure out how to break.

Thankfully, the car arrived quickly. Layla slid into the back seat, and he got in after her, shutting the door quietly. Layla stared out the window, her face and posture stony.

Zahir looked her up and down a few times. So much for the painstaking progress they'd made as coworkers and friends. Even if every day he allowed himself just a little reverie about their fantastic sex.

A few moments of silence went by, stretching tighter with every second. He couldn't take it anymore. "Have I done something to upset you?"

Her chest heaved, like maybe she hadn't breathed the entirety of the car ride. Layla's grip tightened on the door rest. "I...I don't know why you'd ask that."

"You've been acting strangely around me."

Layla blinked a few times, nibbling on her bottom lip. Finally, she cleared her throat, shifting in her seat. "I just, uh...I don't know."

"It's important to me that we have a good working relationship. And this has not been good, or working." He gestured to the air between them.

Layla's gaze fell to the open seat between them. "I just still find it weird that we work together after...everything that's happened."

Her words tumbled through him like boulders. That was it? "I see. Well, I suppose that could be strange for you."

The sound of the car's turn signal was the only sound between them for a moment. "Have you slept with everyone at the office?"

She asked it casually, as if maybe she were asking about what time a play began.

He knitted his brows together. "No, of course I haven't. That's absurd." He huffed with a disbelieving laugh. "No animal shits where they eat."

Layla's gaze scorched over him. "So that's what it was? Fucking me was shitting?"

The fire in her tone prickled at him, sent his frustration tumbling over the edge. "Oh, come on! Of course not. That's not what I meant at all. What are you getting at with this?"

She shrugged, her nostrils flaring as she turned back to stare out the window. "Just trying to figure out how you feel about it."

"How could I have known who you were, that you would end up at my company?" His voice tightened with anger. "Do you make it a habit of sleeping with your bosses?"

Her mouth fell open, shock rippling across her face. "How dare you suggest that!"

"But don't you see that—"

"Let me out." She grabbed at the door handle, but it was locked. The car moved too fast to step out of, even if she was bolstered by anger. "I don't want to hear any more of this. I'll walk."

"You will not walk," Zahir countered, leaning toward her. "This neighborhood is too dangerous for a woman at night."

"Oh well. I have mace." She unbuckled her seat belt, speaking to the driver. "Excuse me, sir? Could you drop me off here?"

Zahir sent her a sharp look and addressed the driver in Farsi. "Continue to her building."

Layla leaned back into her seat, crossing her arms over her chest.

"And buckle up. I'm taking you home. There's no need to be so...adversarial. You weren't like this before."

Her face darkened. "Before?"

"Yeah. Back when you acted like you liked me. When you'd let me lead. I can't even believe now that you let me touch you."

She glowered out the window, tight-lipped. He ran a hand through his hair, heart beating wildly. He hadn't meant to say all those words...but they were out now. No turning back.

A few moments later the car slowed as they approached her building. "This is me," she said, her voice monotone.

When the car rolled to a stop, Zahir reached for the door handle. "I'll let you out."

She scoffed, and by the time he'd crossed the back of the car, she was pushing out of the car on her own. He clenched his jaw, meeting her fiery gaze. There was something mischievous there. Yes, she was provoking him. The energy crackled plainly between them.

"I don't need a man to help me out of the car," she spat and strutted past him into the building. He balled his fists, stilling his hand. He could have grabbed her by the wrist, spun her around, pinned her to the trunk of the car. Pressed himself against her, asked her if what she really needed was a man to make her feel better. In a way only he could. The image passed before his eyes like a movie, and by the time he could clear his head, she was inside the building, heading for the elevator.

He swore to himself, lingering at the side of the car. The woman in that car wasn't even a little bit the Layla he'd come to know over the past month. Something was seriously wrong—and more than that, he could taste the desire that dripped from her like honey. She might play this part, but it wasn't working. She needed him—maybe as a friend or maybe as a lover. Either way, he needed to show up.

Zahir poked his head into the car. In Farsi, he said, "Park the car. I'll let you know soon if I'll be coming down."

He hurried into the building, murmuring the apartment number to himself. He'd helped secure this spot, so he knew exactly what apartment was hers. Sixth floor, number 621. A three bedroom with a hot tub and balcony. He'd opted for something a bit more luxurious than he otherwise might have, since he'd known it would be hers.

He tapped his thumb against the elevator panel as the car rose toward the sixth floor, as though the motion might help alleviate some of the tension in his chest. There was no good reason to go up to her apartment, other than his desperation for her. He wanted to take her into his arms and feel that tension melt away, get back to their witty rapport, smooth out whatever this uncomfortable kink was between them.

When he found her door, he took a deep breath before knocking, not allowing any doubts to creep in and remind him what a bad idea this might be.

He was following his gut, and it told him to go after her.

CHAPTER ELEVEN

Layla leaned against her front door for what felt like an hour, chest heaving as she struggled to rid herself of the memory of Zahir's heated gaze. What the fuck had just happened between them? It was like teenage rebellion mixed with professional suicide. And there she was, trapped in the middle, desperate to let him in but terrified to admit the truth.

She smoothed her palms against the cool door behind her, replaying the evening in her head. This would make work awkward as hell from now on. She hadn't intentionally wanted to ruin things between them. But on the other hand, the only way forward might be ruining their sexual attraction. There was just no happy medium with Zahir. She needed all of him or nothing.

Just come back, Zahir. She squeezed her eyes shut, feeling tears prick her eyes. She wanted him in a way she could scarcely understand, much less rationalize. But his warmth by her side, the steadiness of his energy…god, that would help right about now.

Knock knock knock.

She jolted, spinning to face the door. It was nearly eight p.m. Nobody visited her without calling first. And her only real visitor was Marian, who had gone home with Omar.

Knock knock.

She gulped, tongue sticking to the roof of her mouth, and peered through the peep hole. Zahir stood on the other side, a hand propped up on the doorframe outside. He looked wrecked, gnawing at the inside of his lip.

Holy shit. Holy shit. Her heart raced as she contemplated a plan. But what could she do? She'd come apart with him inches away, inside her own living space. This was doomed. And in a way…she was grateful for it.

She tugged open the door, a shocked silence passing between them. Their eyes locked, Zahir looking at her as though searching for permission to come in. She didn't move—couldn't move, when those obsidian eyes absorbed every last ounce of her willpower. Her breaths turned sharp and shallow.

"Layla," was all he said.

She grabbed his wrist, bringing him inside the apartment. He kicked the door shut behind him, his warm, rough hands cupping her cheeks. Her eyes fluttered shut, whimpering against the tenderness, relief washing through her.

"I needed to make sure you were okay." His arms slid around her waist, bringing her against him. She palmed the flat planes of his chest, head spinning.

"I wasn't." Her forehead dropped to his chest. "But I am now."

His breath came out hot by her ear. She clutched at the front of his shirt, letting the slow washes of desire consume her. Heat singed her, burned away the last of her resistance. He'd shown up, despite her shitty attitude, despite her coldness. And god, it felt like a sign. At the very least, a sign that it was time to just give in to all the feelings she'd been battling for the past few weeks. Let go of the confusion of the test result, abandon all the what-ifs and what-nows.

Zahir would be her release. The only one she craved.

His hand smoothed over the curve of her jaw, nudging her head back. She looked up at him, drinking in the intensity of his gaze, the dark stubble on his jaw, the tiny mole on his cheekbone.

"So can I come in?" He smiled devilishly, which made her giggle. His lips smashed against hers then, a needy kiss quaking between them, causing a low, strangled moan to erupt from her, one she didn't even recognize.

Zahir cupped the sides of her head as they kissed, one kiss bleeding into another. Her lips tingled, body on fire. *This.* This is exactly what she'd needed, the entire damn time. Denying it was a sin, one that she was forced to commit for the sake of her job. But tonight, it didn't matter.

They stumbled into her apartment, Layla leading them blindly toward the couch. They reached the edge and she fell backwards, laughing as her ass met the soft cushion. Zahir stood above her, commanding and dark, his gray slacks bearing a telltale ridge in the crotch.

"Work used to be easy for me," Zahir said, his eyes on his shirt cuffs as he unbuttoned each wrist. His thick fingers moved to his shirtfront then, undoing each button in turn. "But now, it's fucking torture. Because every day, you're there. In the office next to me. And I can't touch you or kiss you or do fucking anything."

She gaped at him as he spoke, entranced by the caramel flesh of his arms as he shrugged his shirt off.

"Do you like this game we've been playing?" His belt buckle clanked as he tore the leather strap through the loops. "Is it fun for you to pretend like we're just colleagues?"

She swallowed hard, unable to move her gaze from the waistband of his briefs as he pushed his pants down. He was almost completely nude in front of her and she couldn't even concentrate long enough to undress.

"I...I wouldn't say it's fun," she started.

"No. It's hell." He tossed his clothes aside, his cock leaning hard against the fabric of his briefs, making an impressive tent. "Put me out of my misery, Layla. In the way only you can."

His words shivered through her, reminding her to move. Yes, a gorgeous, sculpted god was in front of her, asking her to disrobe.

She had to comply immediately. With shaky fingers, she unbuttoned her blouse, breath hitching as Zahir knelt in front of her on the couch, sliding it over her shoulders. She undid her pants and shimmied out of them, letting Zahir slide them down her thighs and over her ankles, slipping off her heels in the process.

When she was clad only in her bra and panties, Zahir hummed low, his long fingers digging into the flesh of her hips.

"I've been waiting for this," he murmured, lips grazing the tops of each breast. Her legs fell open, neck limp to the side.

"Me too," she whispered, hardly able to find her voice. Waiting for it was an understatement. She'd been unable to function without it.

Zahir tugged down the cups of her bra, her breasts bouncing out. She sucked at her teeth as he took each nipple between his lips. His kisses moved downwards, over the curve of her low belly, leaving a moist trail. He nuzzled the damp crotch of her panties, his eyes glinting black as he peered up at her.

"I wish I could do this to you every day." His gravelly voice made goosebumps flare all over her body.

"That doesn't seem like such a bad idea," she said, watching as his thick fingers slid beneath the fabric of her panties. He pushed it aside, his tongue dancing torturously over her swollen lips. She went rigid beneath him, breath caught in her throat.

"Mmm." He flattened his tongue against her clit, sending a shock wave through her. Her hand wandered to his head, fingers tightening in the thick mess of hair she imagined touching every goddamn day at work. Why did he have to be perfect? As a coworker, he was impossible to ignore. As a man, he was everything she'd ever fantasized about.

He dragged a thumb over her dripping entrance, taking a bite of the soft flesh of her inner thigh. Zahir rubbed his jaw over the place he'd just bitten, his stubble scratching lightly. She inhaled sharply as he pressed a finger inside her. His eyes were intense on her as he pumped the finger in and out, the thumb of his other hand making slow, deliberate circles around—not across—her clit. He was teasing her. And too well.

"God, Zahir," she groaned, tossing her head back. "Just make me come already."

He shook his head, circling that needy nub like it was his prey. "Not yet."

"I need it."

The corners of his mouth turned up. "I know you do. And you'll get it."

She whimpered, arching toward him, desperate to feel any contact against her throbbing clit. His finger felt glorious inside her but it wasn't enough, it provoked more than it sated. She tightened the fist in his hair, bucking against him.

Zahir brushed his lips ever-so-lightly over her clit, enough to make her groan. Fuck, he was good at pushing her buttons. Her legs splayed wider, the grin on his face growing more devilish.

"Come on," she urged.

"In time," he murmured, kissing the stubbly mound of her mons. He'd slipped a second finger inside her, almost without her realizing, the pumping becoming more forceful. One of his hands snaked up to her breast, tweaking a nipple. She gave a strangled cry.

And while her head was tossed back, Zahir dove in. He poked and prodded her clit with his tongue, lavishing upon it all the attention she'd craved. She went rigid, hesitant to move in fear that it might end. Zahir moaned as he slurped at her clit, his tongue dancing expertly over the tight nub. She clenched her thighs around his head as the tension inside her climbed.

He pulled back after a moment, his mouth shiny.

"What are you doing?" She grabbed at his shoulder, urging him between her legs.

He sent her a flat look, reaching for his pants. "I need to be inside you." He rummaged through his pockets, and then produced his wallet. He fished out a condom, then pushed his briefs down. His chest heaved as he rolled the condom over his cock.

"Yes," she whispered, unable to look away from the veiny, purplish head, his cock arching gently up into the air in front of him. Even his penis was perfect. Like it belonged in a magazine. Or at least as the textbook example of aroused genitalia.

He slipped his wide, warm hands beneath her ass cheeks, hoisting her into the air. His cockhead slipped back and forth across her entrance, and then with a measured thrust he sunk inside her, his gaze never wavering from hers. Her breath shriveled in her throat as he disappeared inside her, his heat reaching all the way to her core.

"Fuck," she gasped, clinging to his forearms. He pulled back and then thrust inside her, steady and forceful, stretching her, sending electricity zipping through her limbs.

His jaw clenched as he pumped into her, gaze never wavering. The muscles of his belly flinched as he worked her, his fingers leaving indents in the sides of her hips.

"Don't stop," she breathed, locking her legs around him. With each withdrawal, she was seconds closer to coming, the tension thick and spring-loaded inside her. She'd been fantasizing about him since the day they met, but nothing satisfied her like Zahir himself.

Zahir drilled into her again, rocking his hips in a slow circle once he was buried to the hilt. She gasped into his shoulder, biting at the warm skin there, and he nuzzled the hollow of her neck. Their lips met a moment later, a frenzied, passionate kiss emerging, something raw and real that made tears well up in the back of her throat. Without breaking the seal of their kiss, he rocked against her, pressing himself so deep that she moaned.

He pinched one of her nipples, rolling it between his fingers, thrusting into her so deep that she saw stars. She fell over the edge then, a quaking, messy tumble of sparks and hot rushes. She clung to his strong neck, letting out a low, warbling moan that sounded like it came from someone else. Pleasure wracked her body, pussy clenching in waves around him as he drew back again and then thrust deep. A moment later he grunted and stilled.

Her vision went spotty for a moment until the pleasure receded, allowing her to think straight again. Chest heaving, she dragged her lips along the salty skin of his collarbone, hesitant to break the reverie of the climax.

"That," she said after a few moments, the silence broken only by their satisfied, heavy breaths, "that is really hard to say no to."

CHAPTER TWELVE

They lounged on her couch, half-nude and relaxed, for longer than Zahir realized. By the time he thought to check his phone, an hour had gone by in comfortable conversation and lighthearted laughter.

"If you keep sitting with these out," Zahir smoothed his hand over the lush curve of her breast, "we'll be forced to start round two."

"Forced, huh?"

He smiled as she stood up, squeezing his shoulder on her way to the kitchen. She came back with a pitcher of water and two glasses. "Water? I also have wine."

"No. I just want you." He hooked her at the waist, bringing her down onto his lap. She giggled, rubbing her butt against his groin as she settled into place.

"Is this how we should work from now on?" She glanced back at him, mischief on her face. "We can just merge our offices. I'll sit on top of you in all meetings."

He laughed. "That would be my dream come true."

She poured two glasses of water from her perch on his lap while thoughts about work began skulking through his mind.

"You know…" he said after a moment.

"What?" She turned, handing him a glass.

"What happened tonight…and before…" He sipped at his water, feeling suddenly parched. "I needed it then, and I needed it now."

"Me too," she said in a small voice.

"I'm going to keep needing it, too." He squeezed her left hip with his free hand.

She smirked, looking back at him. "What are you getting at?"

"I don't want to keep playing this game. This thing between us can't be ignored." His heart raced while he spoke, like the mere words uncorked a well he hadn't been expecting. Heat rushed through him. "But I don't want to lie or lead you on, either."

She turned on his lap, her legs hanging over the side of the couch. "Okay."

"I have…obligations," he said, his neck heating at the mere reference to his pending marriage. "To my family and to the company. So, I wouldn't expect you to, you know…" He waved his hand in the air. This was delicate territory, and he wanted to avoid it altogether. "I don't see this going away. But I also see that it has a natural limit."

Her face went stony, which sent a pang of fear through him. "Right."

"Am I making sense?"

She turned to him, a bright smile coming over her face. "Perfect sense. Thank you."

He paused, trying to feel her out. It was as clear as he could make it—please be with me as long as possible, before I sign my life away to a woman I don't even know.

"But I can understand too if this might be uncomfortable. I'd be willing to help you achieve whatever arrangement fits best. Moving to a different department, relocation…in the event that you decide you, well, don't want to continue."

"Zahir." She slung her arms around his neck, her face growing stern. "I'm a liberated western woman, remember? You don't have to worry this much."

He nodded, taking another gulp of water. He should have known. Besides, it was clear this meant more to him than it did to her, especially since the only people who knew about his upcoming betrothal were his brothers and father. She had no way of knowing that their liaisons were *destined* to end. No matter how much he wanted to continue seeing her, getting to know her, planting those sweet kisses all over her face…

Layla finished her glass of water and stood, heading for the far corner of the room. She bent to pick something up, exposing the shiny redness of her pussy. Zahir's jaw clenched when he realized she had his briefs dangling from her fingertips.

"Here's your underwear…unless you'd prefer to remain nude on my couch for just a little while longer," she purred, easing down next to him.

He set his glass on the table beside the couch, then tugged her down on top of him by the hips. She laughed, bending her knees to straddle him, her perky breasts nudging him in the face.

"I think I'll stay here until it's absolutely necessary for me to leave," he murmured, placing small kisses along her collarbone. Remnants of his stilted confession to her still rang between his ears, and part of him wished he could confess everything—the betrothal, the sense of helplessness, the fact that the only woman he was truly, deeply interested in was *her*.

But those doubts were swept away by a maelstrom of kisses and gentle touches, until all that remained was the throbbing echo of *Layla*, playing like a mantra in his head.

*   *   *

The next few weeks passed as a blur before Zahir's eyes. After that night in Layla's apartment, they fell into a tacit, easy rhythm. One that required almost no thought, just simple, heated glances and the perfectly-timed head nod to indicate "meet me in my office" or "follow me to the boardroom."

The two of them fucked everywhere. In their offices, on top of the desk, bent over the chair, in the boardroom after work hours, even inside one of the bathrooms in the early morning hours. Zahir ate her out whenever he could, and she'd given him more blowjobs than he could count. The risk of being discovered weighed on him—was more of an anxiety than anything else—but he couldn't control himself either. He was a man unhinged. Crazed for Layla. Desperate to absorb as much of her as he could while he still had the chance.

He'd never been so buoyant at work. His secretary mentioned something once, that he had a special glow. It was a sex glow or a Layla glow—or both. Either way, it was obvious to the outside world; he felt compelled to squash it but helpless to stop. Was it so wrong to be enjoying this so much?

Besides, he and Layla had reached a new level between them. It was effortless, something sweet and playful that he would have no problem continuing for a long time. Their workday romps weren't quite enough, but they satisfied him—temporarily, at least. He wanted more of her. Outside of work. In his penthouse, at her apartment, at dinner, maybe even weekend trips.

You want Layla. The thought sizzled through him as he reviewed his emails one Friday, something both obvious but much deeper than simple wanting. Of course he wanted her. He'd wanted her since the day he met her. But this was something else. He wanted her *for his own.* His mystery bride and upcoming wedding weighed on him like a lead jacket, an oppressive future that sometimes had him waking up at night unable to breathe.

Zahir checked his watch. A few hours left in the day. He'd been considering his weekend plans, trying to find a casual way to insert Layla into them without coming off as overbearing. But at this point, he should go for it. Just ask her to dinner. What was the harm? He could pass it off as a business meeting easily enough…or invent a story about how they'd run into each other unexpectedly on solo excursions out on the town. Either way, he had leverage now to deal with speculation from errant reporters or press hounds. He could easily deflect them to research her status within the company.

Toward the end of the day, his father called. Zahir cradled the phone between his ear and shoulder as he reviewed some reports. "Father."

"My son, I have some news for you." His father's voice had that unnerving joviality again. Zahir's stomach shrank to a nut.

"What is it?" He stopped seeing the screen, even though he was staring at it.

"We've set a date." His father's glee rumbled through the phone. "Set by the bride's family. Five months from now."

Zahir blinked, nearly dropping the phone. He caught it as it slid away from his face. "What? That…it seems…"

"Don't worry, you'll meet her soon enough." He could practically see his father waving away his concerns. "She finishes her master's degree in two months and then will come home to prepare for the wedding. I imagine we'll have quite a party planned for that time, as well."

Zahir's mouth went dry. Two months until he met her. Five months until married. It all seemed so fast…and unpalatable. "Father, are you sure—?"

"What, son?"

"Are you sure this isn't a little fast?" He blinked rapidly, trying to piece together some sort of logical protest. One that didn't reek of the fact that he wanted to sidestep the marriage altogether. "I mean, usually there's at least a year to prepare. I hardly think we can throw an appropriate wedding in so little *time*."

His father hummed on the other end of the phone. "Yes, you may be right. It does seem fast. But this is the date the bride's family has chosen. They have final word in these matters."

Zahir pinched his eyes shut. There was no way out. "Thank you for the update, Father. Very good news." His stomach clenched as he said it.

"Indeed, it is!" His father hung up, practically buzzing with happiness. Zahir stared at his computer screen, hesitant to breathe or blink or do anything that might let this reality sink deeper into him than it already was.

Two months to introduction; five months to marriage. It translated in his head to *no more Layla.* And that stung worse than anything.

Now that there was a date set, he and Layla's end was in sight. He had to come clean about the marriage, and his future…eventually. Because shouldn't he also enjoy what little time remained between them? Two more months at least were better than no more months.

But the thought of telling Layla wrung out his insides. On the one hand…she might not care. Might toss her hair and say "oh well" and want to keep fucking up until the last hour before his wedding. Or maybe she'd be angry or even feel betrayed. He'd prefer the latter to the former.

Because there was no way around it: he and Layla had something between them. Even though it was disguised as work fun, there was more there. And if it turned out Zahir was the only one wrapped up in this fantasy…

That was something he was willing to postpone finding out about.

CHAPTER THIRTEEN

Layla stood in front of her bedroom mirror, inspecting herself from all angles. How far along was she now? It was hard to tell, since she refused to visit the doctor quite yet. Morning sickness had set in for real, and by her count, it had probably been around fourteen weeks since her last period—she'd been in Parsabad for three months now. But an ultrasound seemed out of the question. Not yet. Not while things still seemed relatively normal.

Am I showing yet? She squinted, twisting to check out her belly from the side. Could Zahir notice anything? He certainly hadn't seemed to notice anything amiss over the last four weeks of non-stop fooling around. The doorknob jiggled, but she didn't glance at the doorway. Marian stepped in a moment later, holding up a taupe set of Spanx.

"Here they are." She waved them in the air. "Flown in especially for you from the US."

"You act like you didn't just order these online," Layla said with a smirk. She snatched them out of her friend's hands, tugging at each side to test the elasticity. "God. I might never fit into these. What size is this, a small?"

"No, it's *your* size. It's just meant to, you know, keep everything in." Marian shrugged, sitting on the bed. "Try them on."

"I'll need an army of women to get into these once I start growing."

"You'll get used to it. It'll become second nature."

"Maybe I'll just put them on once and not take them off again until I deliver," Layla said, stepping one foot tentatively into the opening of the undergarment.

"Listen, this is a *temporary* solution," Marian said, slicing her hand through the air. "You asked me to help, and I did. This is the best I've got while you make up your mind about telling Zahir."

"I already made up my mind," Layla reminded her, guiding her other foot through the opening. She tugged them up until they met resistance mid-thigh. "I've told you. He doesn't need to know."

Marian sighed dramatically. "I just think you need to consider this decision further."

"Why? So I can ruin his family?" Layla scoffed, but it turned into a huff as she struggled to raise the garment higher. "I'm not going to be the black sheep here. It's one thing for me to come around to being a mother. But I refuse to be someone's obligatory wife."

Marian watched flatly through the mirror as Layla tugged the pants higher. "He wouldn't marry you just because he got you pregnant—"

"Oh really?" Layla laughed sarcastically. "You said yourself this is the most traditional family you've ever seen. I can just imagine the scandal his bastard baby would create."

Marian picked at a nail, her mouth a thin line. "Well, I'm sure you two could work something out..."

"Yeah, and he'd have all the leverage. Compared to him, I'm just some broke girl from New York. Who's going to win that custody battle, Mare? Not me, that's for damn sure." Layla grunted. The torture device didn't want to crest her hips, no matter how hard she tugged. "Can you give me a hand?"

Marian hopped to her feet, pulling up at the back of the waistband. Layla wiggled around until the Spanx finally slid into place. She heaved a sigh of relief, assessing herself in the mirror.

"Well at least I can still *breathe*," she said, examining her body again for any evidence of a bump. "Though I might need to have Zahir cut me out if we ever hook up while I'm wearing them."

"I can't imagine your baby growing up not knowing who their daddy is," Marian said, sounding pitiful.

"I know. I know." Layla shook her head. "But if I tell him, and we don't come to the magical perfect agreement in life, then what? Besides, I don't want to settle down. I don't want to live here forever. Zahir's focus is clear—he's strapped to Almasi-Thomas until the day he dies. If I'm attached to him via this baby, I'll be forced to stay here with him. I already know it."

"I think you should tell him," Marian said, gripping her friend by the hips. "I just know that he'd want to know."

Layla deflated a little. "I get it. And I promise I'll think about it. I just...can't decide yet. I'm still wrapping my head around everything." She blinked rapidly, a knot appearing in her throat. Probably a sign of the pregnancy. "There's just so much to think about, you know?"

Marian nodded, her curls bouncing. "I know, honey. I support you in whatever decision you make."

"And please, *don't* tell Omar. If Zahir doesn't know, nobody can know," she said, meeting her friend's gaze hesitantly. It was a tall order. A seriously big request to make of someone. But for now, it was the only decision that felt right. Marian was by her side in this, come hell or high water.

"I promise," Marian said quietly.

"Now. Let's see." Layla turned to her reflection in the mirror once more. "Am I showing or not?"

Marian bit her lip, shaking her head slowly. "Not yet...but when you do, this will hide it."

Layla frowned. "Well, it looks like the Spanx era will soon be upon us."

Marian stayed to hang out and chat a bit longer, as well as to help tug Layla out of the skin-tight Spanx, which helped Layla ignore the insistent pinging of her phone. By the time Marian went home to meet Omar for dinner, Layla realized Zahir had been texting her the whole time. Urgent, fun, and playful texts, imploring her to let him take her out to dinner.

A grin covered her face as she responded. "Dinner? Again? You've taken me out every weekend. Shareholders are going to start thinking you're banging your subordinate."

Little dots let her know Zahir worked on a response immediately. *"But we do so much more than mere banging. So yes? Dinner?"*

She smoothed a hand over the Spanx as she contemplated her reply. Of course she wanted to go to dinner. These last four weeks had been magical and fulfilling in a way she hadn't expected. More than anything, she wanted to continue this fantasy where she and Zahir had pure, unadulterated fun with one another, where they were able to connect and just be together without any consequences. She excelled at this kind of relationship.

Except her guilt at knowing that it was all a ruse gnawed more on her daily. She would be showing soon, for fuck's sake. She couldn't keep up this deception for much longer. She had to tell him.

Marian is right. He needs to know. All of her protests and excuses for keeping it to herself withered when she burrowed down to her gut instinct. And when she got down that deep, another niggling truth emerged. She wanted him to be excited. She wanted him to want *her*. In a way that she was scared to allow herself to crave.

She took a shaky breath. So she'd tell him tonight...come hell or high water. She typed out a quick response. *"Okay. You win. Tell me where and when and dress code."*

She checked herself out in the mirror once more. She'd have to tell him soon...because otherwise, he'd notice himself soon enough. The Spanx would only hide the growing midsection for so long. And sure, she could pawn it off as weight gain for a time...but when the questionable girth turned into that obvious bump?

Her days were numbered.

She nodded at her reflection, offering a small smile for encouragement. *You can do this, Layla. It's time to tell Zahir the truth.*

CHAPTER FOURTEEN

Zahir adjusted the silverware of his place setting for the hundredth time. He'd chosen a fancier place than normal for this dinner—another ostensible business meeting, according to his phone calendar—and it was important that the setting was right. This dinner was more than just another excuse to see Layla's face and hear her snort-laugh at his bad jokes and burn from her alluring looks when he rubbed her leg under the table.

He was confessing tonight, too. The guilt was eating him up.

His assumption that having fun with Layla in the background of his brewing nuptials would be fine had proven naïve. He hadn't counted on things blossoming like they had, their friendship and intimacy a multi-layered zinnia sprawling outward toward the sun. The more time they spent together—whether fucking, fondling, or just talking on the phone late at night—the more Zahir spiraled into conflict.

He wasn't scheduled to meet his bride for another month. But if he waited that long, as he'd originally planned, the situation would only get worse. As it was, it perplexed him at night, keeping him up longer than he wanted.

If you tell her, you know she'll stop seeing you.

This thought plagued him, and he had an arsenal of rationalizations ready. Reasons why she could continue to see him up until his wedding day. They were desperate and foolish, and he knew it. But it was his only option; the only intersection of doing the right thing with his embarrassingly unmanageable desires.

Maybe part of his confession this evening would involve something other than the upcoming wedding. He'd considered it a few times—telling her plainly that he felt more for her than just a work fling, or whatever classification they might use. *This is more than just sex.* The words elbowed for room inside his head when he least expected it. And if he had any choice in the matter, he knew who he'd want to have at his side.

Zahir licked his lips, searching the restaurant for any sign of her. What did he expect her to say? The conversation couldn't end well. Yet he couldn't lose her. He needed every last possible second with Layla.

And you think you won't need her once you get married?

He'd need her more than ever then—he knew it down to his bones. He huffed, adjusting his jacket. These never-ending, circling thoughts wouldn't rest until he reached some sort of peace with the situation. But it might never come.

Layla breezed through the foyer of the restaurant, entering the main dining room like an angel strutting the catwalk. She glowed—she truly did. He smiled, as he always did when he saw her, even when he tried not to. Her face lit up when her gaze landed on him. She glided toward him in a form-fitting black and white dress, something that hugged her curves but left enough to the imagination. He stood as she approached, then pressed a hand to her lower back as she leaned in for a polite kiss on the cheek per custom.

"You look amazing," he murmured into her ear, sideswiped by the rush of heat when he caught a whiff of her perfume. That smell could bring him to his knees.

"Business dinners are important." She winked at him as she sat down, setting her purse in the empty chair at the table. "This one seemed especially urgent. Is the company going through another merger?"

He grinned, leaning back in his chair as a waiter appeared to take her order. She asked for a water with lime.

"No wine?" He reached for the wine list. "I saw a red that I thought we might try."

"No thanks," she said, waving her hand. "I'm not really feeling it tonight."

"All right." He set the list down, settling into seat. "No wine then."

She smiled mysteriously at him. "Why order fancy wine when I can get drunk on you?"

"Am I that fine?"

She hummed. "The finest."

The waiter returned with her water, and she sipped at it while perusing the menu. Zahir watched her read, fascinated by the shine of her hair, the way her eyebrow creased, the quiet way she repeated foreign words as she came across them.

As she decided on her entrée, Zahir mulled over when to tell her. It had to be tonight, that much was certain. But before dinner? During dessert? If he told her and she reacted poorly…shouldn't she eat first before getting upset? There was too much to consider.

Once they'd placed their orders and they found themselves in a pleasant silence, grinning at one another like fools, he realized the truth. He loved this woman.

"Are you okay?" She arched a brow, sipping at her water. "You just got flushed."

"Yeah." He tugged at his collar. He couldn't lose her. "I think it's because I'm hungry."

"Don't fill up here," she said, her voice lowering. She leaned closer over the table. "I've got dessert between my legs."

He leaned closer, capturing her hand in his. Rubbing his thumb over her knuckles, he watched as her expression went from sultry to shocked. He dropped her hand, leaning back in his seat.

"I forget there are eyes when I'm with you," he said, tugging at his collar again. "We should start ordering in."

Their conversation took a turn toward the lighthearted and easy. By the time dinner came, there still wasn't a natural way to bring up his pressing news. They devoured eggplant and fresh hamour fish, and once the plates were cleared, Zahir's heart hammered in his chest. *It has to be now.*

"You know, Layla…there's something I wanted to talk to you about." He sipped at his water, mouth suddenly dry.

"What is it?"

"I'm not really quite sure how to say it." He studied the tablecloth, as though it might offer a clue. *Fuck.*

"I have something to share with you, too. But you go first," she said, nibbling on her bottom lip.

Curiosity streaked through him. What did she want to tell him? Could she possibly feel the same way about him? "I, uh…" His voice evaporated.

"Go on," she said.

"I'm engaged," he blurted, the words falling from his lips like boulders. He searched her face for a reaction, unnerved by the stoniness he saw there. Silence stretched between them for miles. The noise of the restaurant around them shrank to a dull murmur.

"What?"

"My father has arranged a marriage for me," he said quietly, squeezing his hands together under the table.

"How long have you been engaged?" Her question came at him like a javelin.

He winced. "Over a month."

"Jesus Christ," she said, pinching the bridge of her nose. "So I've been the other woman?"

"No. You haven't."

"How could I not be?" She nearly barked the question.

"I don't even know this woman," he said, desperate to make her understand. "I've never met her. That's how these things work."

"Does it matter how they work?"

"Yes, I think so." He blinked rapidly, his stomach sinking slowly to the tips of his toes. Yes, this was going just as badly as he'd imagined.

"Maybe it matters to you, but really? It doesn't matter at all." She slammed her fist on the table, the water in her glass sloshing. "You're engaged to a woman you've never met, but you're fucking me on the regular. So are these dinner dates just some way to thank me for my time while we wait for you to say your vows?"

His breath slithered out of him in one long, low exhale. "That's not what this is—"

"How could it be anything else?" Her voice came out pinched, like she was fighting tears. "You know, I've had fun with you, but not enough fun to abandon my morals." She pushed back in her chair, her mouth a frighteningly thin line.

"Where are you going?"

"I'm leaving," she spat, grabbing at her purse in the extra chair. "I'm not going to participate in this any longer than necessary."

"Layla," he said in a firm voice. "Wait."

"Don't follow me, and don't come to my apartment," she hissed. "I mean it."

"Let's talk this out," he pleaded, grabbing for her wrist. He felt curious eyes whip their way, drawn to the quietly heated exchange. They had to avoid a spectacle. At all costs.

"And reach what conclusion? That you're still getting married to someone else?" She scoffed, shaking her head. "You know, why even bother with me if you knew where this was headed?"

Layla spun on her heel and stormed out of the restaurant, drawing plenty of gazes along with her. Zahir clenched and unclenched his fists, watching her leave. He wouldn't run after her—he knew what that would earn him. Drama and maybe even a fresh slap, not to mention plenty of newspaper coverage.

The waiter returned cautiously. No doubt he'd been observing this from somewhere else. He left the bill, which Zahir paid without even digesting the amount.

As he waited for his credit card to be returned, his mind swirled with protests and ideas. She needed time to cool off. She had to come around. This wouldn't be the end. But how could she just leave like that? What could he do now? His insides felt scrambled and weak as he received his credit card from the waiter, thanking him listlessly.

Zahir stood and left the restaurant, avoiding eye contact until he was out of the building. As he waited for his car, he sucked deep breaths of the evening air, trying like hell to stave off the desperation making predatory steps around him. He couldn't go home, that was for sure. There he'd fall into a sinkhole of self-pity, and maybe even whisky. But where?

He fished his phone out of his pocket, and his fingers maneuvered automatically to Layla's message thread. He typed out a quick message. *"I told you because I didn't want to keep this from you. Please let me explain more."*

A response came quick. *"Fuck you."* A moment later, another message arrived. *"And fuck off."*

Zahir clenched his jaw, swiping away from the messages quickly. That hurt more than he wanted to admit. And in times like these…only one man could help.

He dialed Omar's number. "Brother? I need to come over. There's an emergency."

"Of course," Omar responded. "I'm home. Come now."

On the way to his brother's penthouse, Zahir pinched his eyes shut, letting himself drown in the frustrating blackness of this situation. Layla was the only woman he'd ever been with who made him feel both challenged yet comfortable; aroused but also clear-headed. He wouldn't ever tire of being with her. Simply looking at her brought him more joy than he'd thought possible.

Yes, he was in love.

He slammed his fist against the door handle, sulking as the car approached Omar's building. Like he needed this now. Of all times in his life to fall in love. Right before his own goddamned wedding. It just didn't make sense, and it certainly wasn't fair.

Omar would know how to handle this. He had to. He was the problem-solver, the only person able to navigate treacherous waters of any sort.

When Zahir arrived at Omar's front door, he knocked until Omar pulled open the door, looking distressed.

"One knock is fine; I was expecting you," he said, stepping aside to let his brother in. "Now what's wrong?"

Zahir ran a hand through his hair, searching the foyer and attached great room for evidence of Marian. "Where Marian?"

"On the phone in the bedroom. I think she's talking to Layla."

"Shit." Zahir heaved a sigh, heading for Omar's liquor cabinet along the far wall. He poured himself a whisky, which he took in one shot, then poured himself another.

"What's going on?"

"Layla and I have been sleeping together." He should have admitted it to Omar sooner, but there was no reason to. Not when he thought, foolishly, that everything would be fine in the wake of the engagement.

Omar snorted. "Well I knew *that*."

"You knew?"

"I suspected. I told you at the business dinner last month I could see it all over your face."

"It started before then," Zahir admitted. He gave the brief history of their unexpected hook-up prior to her job at Almasi-Thomas. "About a month ago, we decided to just go for it. Keep having fun and meeting up, because obviously denying it wasn't working."

"That is never the solution," Omar murmured, pouring himself a whisky. Zahir realized he hadn't offered him one and swore.

"Sorry. I should have made you one." He tipped some of the amber liquid into his mouth, sucking at his teeth. "Anyway, in the meantime, father springs the marriage on me. My original thought was that we could continue anyway. I've never met the woman, and it's not like I'm seeing someone else. So what's the harm? Except tonight I decided I should tell her. Just to clear the air."

Omar tutted. "Let me guess. She didn't take it well?"

Zahir shook his head, wincing against another sip of whisky. "She left the restaurant and told me to fuck off."

Omar stared out at the inky sky of the Minarak night, swirling his own whisky in his glass. "And?"

"And? What do you mean? This is self-explanatory."

Omar smiled mysteriously. "Why would you care about her getting upset? It seemed like a physical arrangement. You've had plenty of those."

"I hurt her. Badly." Zahir downed the rest of his whisky, finally feeling the heat of alcohol in his veins. "And I love her."

Omar nodded as if he'd been waiting for it all along. "There it is."

Zahir groaned, just as Marian came down the hallway. She glanced curiously between the two of them. "Hey, Zahir. What's going on?"

"Nothing. Just work trouble." Omar smiled placidly.

"I fucked things up with Layla," Zahir corrected, shooting a glance at Omar. "I came here for help."

Marian raised her palms in the air. "I know nothing, I say nothing."

"Yeah. I'm sure." Zahir narrowed his eyes at his sister-in-law, pouring another whisky. This had to be his last, or he'd go down a dark path.

"So, will you or will you not marry the girl father chose for you?" Omar's voice was too calm for the strife in Zahir's chest. It irked him.

"Of course I will," he spat, his nostrils flaring. "I have to. There's no other choice."

"You don't have to, you know."

"Yes, I do." Zahir scowled into his glass as he took another sip.

Omar didn't look convinced. "Does it help to know he chose this bride for the company's sake? It's the best *business* move. The bride's family has land that he wants to mine."

Zahir grunted.

"He himself married our mother so that he could drill the fields we now own a stake in." Omar put on an encouraging face, which only made Zahir frown.

"That doesn't make me feel better."

"Then think of this," Omar went on. "Layla is a strong woman. She will recover. She can survive this. You just need to do what's right."

"But maybe the right thing isn't marrying this stranger," Marian countered, her voice edged with something unknown. "How do you know what's best?"

"We all do what is best for the family," Omar said, addressing Marian. "There are no exceptions to this."

Marian's gaze went dark. "Exactly my point."

Zahir blinked at each of them. "What…is going on?"

Marian flipped her hair. "I'm not getting involved. I just think you and Layla need to have a conversation so she can say everything she needs to say."

A frighteningly thick silence settled between them, one that suffocated at the same time it penetrated.

Omar shrugged, a clouded look crossing his face. "There you have it."

Zahir took another sip of his whisky. "She won't let me in if I go there now."

"Then go whenever you can. Tomorrow. The next day. It just has to happen," Marian said.

Zahir nodded, twisting the tumbler in his hand. Marian's vague advice circled awkwardly inside him, trailing something heavy behind it. "You're right." He looked between his brother and sister-in-law, then gave them each a hug. "Thanks for listening. I should really get some sleep."

But sleep wouldn't come. Zahir wasn't dumb enough to expect sleep tonight. All he'd be able to do would be think of Layla and wonder what her unrevealed news might be.

CHAPTER FIFTEEN

First thing Monday morning, Layla marched into Almasi headquarters with resignation papers tucked under her arm.

She'd poured over the document all weekend, as well as cried her eyes out and made peace with the fact that her brief, whimsical brush with feeling something for a man had once again led right where she'd expected: heartbreak.

There was no other way to handle this situation. Zahir was off-limits and had been the entire time. Which meant that this baby was hers and only hers, and she had no reason to go ruining Zahir's new, perfect marriage with a surprise child with some fleeting New Yorker.

Tears welled up in her throat again. Good thing Zahir had shared his news first. One more disaster averted.

Part of her could understand his ridiculous man logic. *Just fuck until I legally wed someone else.* It almost made sense, if you took feelings out of the mix. But what Zahir didn't know, what Layla wouldn't admit under threat of death, was that his confession ruined the tiny, eager sprouting seed of hope within her that what she felt for Zahir was real and might actually go somewhere.

She knocked her head against the side of the elevator, as if it might help loosen the thought so it could roll out of her ear. Don't you understand how hard it is for me to open up? I trusted you. I thought you were special. I thought we had a connection. I dared to hope with you.

She'd been saying these words to him in her head all weekend long. It didn't matter how many times she repeated them. It never hurt any less.

When the elevator doors slid open, she headed straight for Almasi Senior's office. She knocked three times, waited for his rumbly voice, then let herself in.

"Miss Layla." He grinned up at her, eyes squinting. "Everything all right?"

"Yes, sir." She forced a quick smile, handing him the papers. "I just wanted to drop these off. I'm sorry to deliver this news so soon."

His bushy brows furrowed as he read. After a moment, he said, "But I don't understand. Aren't you well paid here?"

"Yes, sir. Very well paid." Her heart picked up a fast rhythm. "It's not the pay, in fact."

"Then what is it? You've only been here three months."

"I, uh, well…" Her palms went clammy as she struggled to remember the monologue she'd practiced at home in the mirror.

132

"You know, this is very far from home and very *different*. I just realized that I should be closer to the people I love." She paused, struggling to remember another convincing reason. "And the weather? It's very hot. I find that it's hard to—"

"It's too hot for you?" His eyebrow arched accusingly as his gaze drifted downward. A thick moment of silence passed. Heat prickled over her neck.

Oh God. Maybe I'm actually showing. She shifted, doubts flooding her. Her mouth started moving but she couldn't control the words. "I've just been very unwell here, actually, feeling sick and sort of, you know, *under the weather,* sort of puking when I wake up and—"

Mr. Almasi's brow arched higher. "Puking?"

"It's sort of a, a—" Her cheeks flamed; this was a train wreck. "A problem that definitely can be resolved, I just need to be closer to home, and with the duration of the illness around nine months I don't think that I can fulfill the year contract."

The silence that filled the room became so loud that her head throbbed. Her heart pounded as she struggled to think back on what she'd even said.

"So you're pregnant," he stated matter-of-factly.

The air whooshed out of her lungs. There was no coming back from this gaffe. "Yes."

"We have an excellent maternity package," Mr. Almasi said, looking almost amused. "There would be no problem for you if you were to stay on."

Her cheeks flushed, and a string of curse words thundered through her head. "Sir, I appreciate that fact, and I do understand that there is a very generous maternity package, but as you can probably guess, I'd like to be closer to home at this time."

The doorknob turned, and the door swung open. Goosebumps flared on her calves and she let her eyes flutter shut, groaning internally. She already knew who it was.

"Father." Zahir's voice flooded her, made her knees weak, and she kept her back as rigid as possible. "Are you busy?"

"Well, yes, a bit, I'd say." Mr. Almasi grumbled a bit, adjusting his position in his seat. "Layla, you'll forgive me for sharing your news so soon, but Zahir is the CEO in training, so he should hear this as well."

"What?" Zahir sent her a hard look.

"I—" Layla began.

"Layla is with child and wishes to resign," Mr. Almasi said, steamrolling her with the admission. Zahir's face tightened slowly, as if someone tugged at his cheeks from behind.

Layla's stomach made a somersault, and she backed toward the door. "Well, that's all for now. Thank you both for a very pleasant time at Almasi-Thomas. I'll go get my things ready now. I'll be leaving within the hour."

She bolted past Zahir, ignoring the heat rolling off of him, the confusion that he wore like a suit. She kept her eyes on the ground as she headed for her own office. A moment later a door slammed behind her and footsteps approached.

"Layla." His voice was firm, quiet.

She swallowed a knot of tears and continued to her office. Head hanging, she pushed inside, tears blurring her vision. She studied her desk top, unable to look up at him, unable to do anything for fear of betraying the emotions holding her hostage right now.

The office door shut a moment later. Nobody spoke, and Layla did her best to calm herself. When she looked up, Zahir's face was unreadable.

"Is it mine?"

Her brain seized, and she got lost in his eyes. Tears returned to her eyes, and a few broke the seal, trickling down her face. She covered her mouth with a hand, trying to stifle a sob. She nodded hard, looking back at her desk.

"Jesus, Layla." He stepped closer, reaching for her over the desk. She shied away, drawing a ragged breath.

"You're the only one," she whispered, and then hiccupped. "The only one I've been with."

Zahir stared at her, a range of emotions playing across his face. But it hurt too much to look at him. It reminded her of all the rationalizing she'd done to get to this point, all the excuses and bad decisions.

"How long have you known?"

She shuddered with another sob. "Since that business dinner. The real one."

His eyes widened, a vein pulsing in his neck. For a moment, she thought he'd put his fist through the desk.

"Are you serious?" His voice held a note of incredulity she hadn't known he was capable of. She nodded, shrinking back.

"And you never thought to tell me?"

"I was going to," she whispered, wiping at her eyes. Her mascara was probably wrecked. Her life was definitely wrecked. "At dinner the other night—"

"I can't believe this." Zahir paced the office, his hands tugging at his hair. She drew another breath, struggling to hold onto the break in tears. "I need to think about this. I can't talk to you right now."

Layla wiped at her eyes, fighting another up-swell of emotion.

"We will discuss this later," Zahir said, stopping in his tracks. He pointed at her, the gesture cementing his words. "You will wait for me, and we will discuss this."

He paused, nostrils flaring, and then let himself out of her office. Layla collapsed into her chair, letting another wave of sobs consume her.

Wait for him to discuss this? She owed him an explanation, that much was certain, but she couldn't be in this building any longer. Once the tears subsided, she scribbled down the admin information for her log-in and gathered the few items she had placed around her desk, pushing them into her purse. And then she scooted out of the office, heading to the elevator, head down and heart splintered.

CHAPTER SIXTEEN

Zahir paced his office enough times to wear a visible track into the carpet. He moved from one end of the office to the other, pausing only to mutter a curse word or groan. Layla was pregnant? And it was his?

He was going to be a *father*?

Nothing made sense, and the more he thought about it, the further he drifted down the path of a decision that had essentially made itself the second his father opened his mouth with the news. He had to call off the engagement. There was no other choice, and that was the most absurd part about it. His father would be furious; the company would suffer. The very two things Zahir lived his life to avoid.

But what else could he do? There was no way he could move forward in life abandoning his unborn child from the get-go. And *Layla.* He couldn't abandon her; had never wanted to in the first place. Every cell in his body craved her, despite the secret-keeping and the turmoil. Even amid the anger and the shock, he wanted to cradle her in his arms, let her know that he was going to take care of everything.

Of course, if he called off the engagement in favor of marrying the foreigner carrying his child, he ran the risk that the board wouldn't accept him as the new CEO. Nothing was set in stone. Zahir stepping up to the plate was more of a ceremonial nod to his father's legacy, but the board could hire a new CEO in a heartbeat if they decided Zahir was a liability.

But screw it. Screw them all. This was a risk he had to take.

Somehow, the anger and the shock made one thing startlingly clear: he loved Layla, and this was the only right move. This was the move he'd wanted to make the entire time. He wanted to choose *Layla.*

Zahir stormed out of his office, emboldened by the decision percolating in his gut. He headed for his father's office, bursting in without knocking. His father looked up with hooded eyes.

"Don't you bring me more bad news," he warned.

"I can't go through with the wedding," Zahir blurted. His father set down his pen very slowly, his gaze narrowing on him.

"What did you say?"

"I don't want to marry her. I can't do it."

"And why can't you?"

"Because I'm in love with Layla and she's pregnant with my child."

His father leaned back into his chair, his face unreadable. The silence that filled the room throbbed between Zahir's ears, each passing second making his heart beat faster.

"Father, say something," Zahir pleaded after what felt like an eternity. Anything, even an angry outburst, would be better than this silence.

His father hadn't moved, remained still as a statue. "Are you sure?"

"Yes," Zahir said, his voice cracking.

"How do you know it's yours?"

"We've been meeting up in secret for months," Zahir said, averting his gaze. There was nothing more embarrassing than admitting his infidelity as a grown man. "It can only be mine."

His father let out a long, raggedy sigh. He covered his face with his hands and stayed there for a long while.

"Father," Zahir started.

"What do you want to do?" His father sat up, sniffing.

Zahir blinked. He'd never been asked that before. His conditioned response was to blurt out *whatever you want*. But that wasn't the truth. It hadn't been for a long time. "I want to be with Layla, the woman that I love. I want to help raise our child. I want to run this company." When another silence descended,

Zahir added, "And I want to honor you. Honor this family and the thousands of people that depend on us."

His father nodded slowly, some of the color finally returning to his face. "Good. That is good." He tapped his finger against the desk. "You are a good son, Zahir."

Zahir's belly twisted. This was certainly unexpected. Had he ever heard those words from his father's lips before? He buried his hands in his pockets, unsure how to respond.

His father sighed and swiveled away toward his computer, waving his hand in Zahir's direction. "Go, now. Just go."

Zahir opened his mouth to ask him to add more, but decided against it. This was his decision, and it would happen without or without his father's approval. He stumbled toward the door, his legs gelatin, feeling more buoyant and bristling than ever before in his life.

*   *   *

Layla rubbed her thumb over the smooth surface of a stone before hurling it into the sea. Marian rubbed her back while she intermittently threw rocks into the water, and murmured softly whenever tears arrived.

"I'm happy you finally did it." Marian leaned her head against Layla. She'd come as soon as Layla called, leaving the office immediately after Layla said the word 'resigned.' "He needed to know."

"Yeah." Layla picked up another rock, examining its dappled surface.

"Omar and I had a lot of rocky territory between us at the beginning, too," Marian went on, squinting out at the sea. The water lapped placidly at the stilts of a nearby dock. They'd met at a public access point a few miles from the Almasi headquarters.

"We don't have rocks," Layla said through a tight throat. "We have a bump. One that angered him, and made him storm out of my office."

Marian stroked her hair. "Well, what did you want Zahir to say? It's big, shocking news. Probably one of the reasons you avoided telling him in the first place."

Layla nodded glumly.

"I'm not judging you for not telling him sooner," she added. "But really. Tell me. If you had imagined some perfect scenario, where it went exactly as you imagined...what would that look like?"

Layla's insides tightened. She was hesitant to even consider it, since her reality was now so far from that silly fantasy.

"I don't know," Layla finally forced out.

"I think you do," Marian said gently. "And I think you're so used to being someone's good time that you forgot to imagine your own happy ending."

"What good is imagining the happy ending?" Layla shot back. "It won't happen. It never does."

"But it does," Marian murmured, squeezing her friend's shoulder. "Even for you. So just imagine it. Come on. What would it look like?"

Layla sighed, adjusting her ass on top of the flat rock. "Fine. Zahir would have been happy, for starters. And he'd..." Layla's throat closed off and she swallowed hard, trying to fight back the tears. "He'd tell me he loves me. Because I'm pretty fucking sure that I love him after all this mess. And he'd say he wants to be with me, to raise our baby, to—" She stopped, tears streaming down her cheek. "He wouldn't marry that dumb girl, and we'd go make a killer apartment somewhere and visit volcanoes on the weekend."

Marian grinned, nodding. "Very good."

"But it's not gonna happen," Layla said, misery slithering back into its rightful spot in her heart.

"You don't know that. But you have to be open to the possibility for it to ever happen in the first place."

Layla sighed, feeling the fight go out of her. She leaned her head against Marian's and let the tears stream down her face until she couldn't cry anymore.

*   *   *

A couple hours later, Marian had returned to the office and Layla sat alone at the sea. Cross-legged with a gentle breeze caressing her, she looked down at her belly, smoothing a hand over the still-invisible bump.

"You'll be my little one," she said, tears instantly filling her eyes. She hadn't cried this much in one day *ever*. Not even when her last boyfriend broke her heart. "I will love you to the moon and back. And whatever happens, you will be safe with me."

She sat for a long time, rubbing her belly, imagining all the sweet things she could show this little creature inside of her. Now that the cat was out of the bag, surely Zahir's family would have some sort of wealthy influence. But that didn't mean that having a baby spelled the end of her life. No, she could travel with the baby to see all the things she'd meant to see alone. She'd pass along that appreciation of the world, of culture, of new experiences.

She could forge a new path, exactly as she saw fit.

She smiled, looking out at the sea. For the first time, the pregnancy felt empowering. She wasn't a helpless bystander or a victim—she was in control of this ship.

"Layla."

She jumped at the unexpected voice and didn't need to turn around to know who it was. Tears came again to her eyes and she stilled. A warm hand rested on her shoulder.

"Baby." Zahir's voice was a balm, one that smoothed everything over with just a couple syllables. She looked up at him through shimmery tears, and the sight of him nearly made her collapse.

"You didn't wait." His voice was chiding, but he smiled a little. He sat on the rock next to her, the scent of his cologne grounding her, bringing her clarity despite the turmoil. She swallowed hard, eyeing his chest, desperate to collapse against him.

"I'm sorry," she said. "I kinda had to get out of there."

"I don't care that you didn't tell me," he said suddenly. "I'm just happy that I know now. And I can take care of you."

She furrowed a brow, looking back at the sea. "But what will your new wife think?"

"I don't have a wife. I only have a girlfriend." He grabbed at her chin, guiding her face back to him.

She avoided his gaze anyway, feeling stubborn. "Oh? Was there another woman on the side you didn't tell me about?"

"Yeah. This strawberry blonde woman from New York." Zahir shifted beside her, leaning closer, his heat flooding her. "Sassy, determined, pretty fertile." He cocked a grin and she couldn't resist. She smiled too.

"She sounds like a bore," Layla said, her throat tightening. "Probably wouldn't want to be with her."

"No, I do." Zahir took her hand in his, sealing her in his grip. "I want to be with her more than anything."

Layla's breath hitched. "How did you find me out here?"

"My spy, Marian." He scooted closer to her.

"What will the board members say?" Her brain swirled like a cyclone. She couldn't believe she even had the capacity to speak right now.

"I have no idea. I'll find out later."

Layla shook with restrained sobs. This was unreal. It was too good to be true. But maybe Marian had been right. She had to be willing to imagine the future before it could even happen.

"Do you even want to be a dad?" Layla swung to look at him, the tender expression on his face slashing her in two.

"I never thought much about it, other than I would know when it was right."

Layla laughed through more tears. "Is this right?"

"The rightest decision I've ever made." Zahir leaned closer, nudging her face with his nose. "Layla, will you be with me? Not in the dark or in secret. Be with me so I can hold your hand in public and we don't care about what the newspapers say."

She drew a raggedy breath. That sounded like heaven. "Yes. And the only difference will be now we won't care about what the newspapers say."

Zahir laughed. "That's right. I held your hand in public already." He ran his fingers up the sides of her arms. "Layla, I love you."

She crumpled into his arms at the words, heat searing through her, making her dizzy and blind. "I love you too, Zahir."

His arms encircled her and she wept into his embrace, relief and adoration sweeping through her. This man, the man she'd been attracted to the second she saw him, was hers in a way she'd been too terrified to even hope for. Their baby had been the greatest blessing of all.

And now all she had to do was take the leap and go with it.

"Where do we go from here?" Layla asked into his chest. "We went from hooking up to coworkers to parents. I can't predict the next step."

"I think it's where you move in," Zahir whispered. "And you wake up at my side every day. And I'll make you breakfast and rub your belly, and we live life exactly how we want."

Layla tilted her head back, getting lost in his gaze, and then pressed her lips to his in a kiss so hard that she saw starbursts.

EPILOGUE

Zahir paced the waiting room of the hospital. Omar gnawed on a fingernail in a chair, while Imaad bounced his knee wildly. Marian leaned against the wall in the far corner, her own belly just starting to show. They'd been occupying various positions in this waiting room for five hours, waiting for some update.

Annabelle arrived a moment later, her arms full of snacks, a delighted look on her face. Her own belly was round and prominent, stretching her sweater thin. "I brought food!"

Imaad grinned, coming up to her. "Are you sure it isn't mostly for you, my dear?"

"Hey. I'm eating for two," Annabelle said, ripping into a chocolate bar.

"And you'll be the next one in there," Marian said, nodding toward the swinging double doors Layla had disappeared behind, hours ago.

"You would have been the first in there," Imaad said.

"Hey, it's not a race," Zahir said sharply, looking at his brothers. "But if it were, I would remind you that I'd be winning."

149

Imaad cracked a grin. "Of course you'd find a way to cheat the standings, brother."

Voices approached the waiting room, followed by a giggle. The brothers turned when their father's trademark rumbling voice sounded. "My sons! And all of their beautiful wives."

His father beamed, on his arm a lithe, dark-haired woman, precisely the woman Zahir had been scheduled to marry. He couldn't have dared dream that she'd have a penchant for older men. It had proved an elegant solution for the company's desire to acquire new drilling lands. Plus, his father was happier than ever. And more than happy to hand over the reins of the business so that he could enjoy this new chapter of his life.

"If it weren't for me, my boys wouldn't be with any of these lovely ladies!" His father grinned at Fahwar, his new wife.

Zahir grinned, rolling his eyes. His father loved to claim responsibility for the rampant success of his sons' love lives.

"Yet we're with them *despite* your matchmaking," Omar quipped.

"Any progress?" He and his new wife settled into a chair nearby. She crossed her legs demurely, leaning into him like a needy kitten.

"Should be an update soon," Zahir said, scrubbing at his stubbly jaw. He hadn't shaved in a full day, not since Layla went into labor. "This baby better come soon."

The double doors swung open, and the doctor approached. A collective gasp rang through the waiting room.

"Mr. Almasi." The doctor smiled at Zahir. "You should come with me."

Zahir stumbled behind the doctor in a daze, his breath caught in his throat. He followed him down a hall to the right and then into a dimly lit room. And there, on a bed, draped in a cream-colored gown, was his beautiful Layla holding a tiny little bundle.

Layla looked up at him, her face red and tear-streaked. "Baby, we have a baby!"

Zahir stumbled closer, his vision shrinking to encompass only them. He brushed Layla's shoulder, then caressed the blanket-swaddled newborn.

"What...?" he began.

"A girl," she choked out. "We have a baby girl."

Zahir felt hot tears sliding down his cheeks, and he pressed his forehead to Layla's while the emotion washed over him, made him stiff and incredulous.

"We should name her after your mom," Layla whispered, holding out the little bundle for him to take. Zahir took his new daughter into his arms, gazing down at her, absorbing her tiny features for the first time.

"Sabella," he whispered. "This is our Sabella."

Zahir leaned forward, hugging Layla while he clutched the baby to his chest. This was his family. The family he couldn't have dreamt of, the family he never realized he needed. His heart was full to bursting, and he showered kisses between Layla and Sabella, the first of the rest of their lives.

These were the girls he'd never let go of.

END OF THE SHEIKH'S PREGNANT EMPLOYEE

ALMASI SHEIKHS BOOK THREE

PLUS: Love your sexy Sheikhs? Keep reading for an exclusive excerpt from Leslie North's bestselling novel, Adjalane Sheikhs Book One, **The Sheikh's Secret Bride.**

THANK YOU!

Thank you so much for purchasing and reading my book. It's hard for me to put into words how much I appreciate my readers. If you enjoyed this book, please remember to leave a review. I want to keep you guys happy! I love hearing from you :)

For all books by Leslie North visit:

Her Website: LeslieNorthBooks.com

Facebook: fb.com/leslienorthbooks

Get SIX full-length novellas by *USA Today best-selling author* Leslie North for FREE! Over 548 pages of best-selling romance with a combined 1091 FIVE STAR REVIEWS! Sign-up to her mailing list and get your FREE books at: Leslienorthbooks.com/sign-up-for-free-books

Sneak Peek

Blurb

Work always comes first for Sheikh Nassir Adjalane. From an early age, he learned business was infinitely more important than having a personal life. But with pressure from an opponent on his board, Nassir suddenly has only one month to marry, or risk being voted out of his company. With everything he's worked toward on the line, Nassir desperately needs a bride…and only one woman will do.

Wedding planner Janna Davis never imagined she'd be summoned to the Middle East to plan Sheikh Nassir's nuptials. But the outrageous sum he's offered will finally give her what she needs to stand on her own two feet. As the planning gets underway, Janna is put off by Nassir's businesslike manner, but she can't deny his appeal. No matter what she's feeling though, Janna has a job to do.

Janna values her independence and refuses to fall for a soon-to-be married man, but what will happen when she learns that she is Nassir's intended bride?

Get your copy of The Sheikh's Secret Bride from

www.LeslieNorthBooks.com

Excerpt

Al-Sarid, Boardroom of Adjalane Oil, three days earlier…

"Nassir, you have disgraced our company," Nimr Adjalane told him, his tone grave.

The fact the oldest member of the board--and his father—was upset meant Nassir hadn't done himself any favors this time. Of course, it didn't help that Nimr had chosen to elect Nassir as CEO over his own brother, Hazim, either.

He should have expected it, he supposed, given the other situations he currently faced. First was the verbal assault debacle with the young woman in Europe. Naturally, the paparazzi had been there to capture every vile exchange then taken every one of them completely out of context.

The young woman involved had been painted as the injured party, when just the opposite was true. She'd thrown herself at Nassir, thrusting her bare breasts in his face, and he'd tried to politely refuse. But when that didn't work and her attempts grew more brazen, he'd resorted to harsher measures, stating he'd rather have sex with a goat than a whore.

Strike one.

Then there were his action in a recent skirmish with the Sharqi Oil Sheikhs. He'd forced the temporary closure of their oil pumping station, then once an agreement had been reached for the purchase of the land beneath the station, attempted to extort a priceless portrait from Amare.

Strike two.

If things did not go well today, this could be counted as the final strike against him.

"Nassir," Nimr, said on behalf of the board. "We have discussed your actions in depth, and believe we have a solution that will not only benefit us, but also the world." Nassir clasped his hands and remained silent. Pride, it seemed, had forced them to take drastic steps to correct what they saw as flaws in his character. Flaws he had no intention of changing "A plan that will improve your reputation both with women and our business partners in the West."

Nassir tapped a finger on the tabletop and waited. He knew he'd crossed the line with the Sharqis and the woman, no matter how well-deserved. But if the board was also trying to appease and attract Western business partners, that did not bode well for him.

"It is our recommendation that you marry."

Marry? Whatever he been expecting them to say, it had not been that.

Nassir opened his mouth to comment, but an angry glare from his father stopped him.

"Our decision is non-negotiable," Nimr said.

Nassir clenched his jaw and lowered his head. Now was neither the time nor the place to fight this battle. That would come later. After the meeting adjourned. "Fine."

"And we are suggesting you find an American bride. This will assure the rest of the world that you are both open-minded and tolerant."

"You can't be serious? My family line has stayed within Al-Sarid for generations."

Nimr stood and slammed his fist down onto the table, "That is irrelevant now. You will marry an American, and you will do so in the next thirty days. Furthermore, you will make amends with the Sharqi family."

"Or what?" Nassir demanded. These men could not be serious.

"Or we will replace you." Nimr narrowed his gaze on Nassir, his voice quiet. "You are cunning and clever. You think there will be a loophole or an exception, but you are wrong."

"Replace me? I am Nassir Adjalane and heir to this empire…"

His father continued despite his protests. "I have taken the liberty of speaking with Taleb Sharqi and he has agreed to help you in this endeavor. You are scheduled to attend Amare's wedding reception tonight. He has already had arrangements to introduce you to several women whom he believes would make a suitable wife." Nimr smiled then, small and cold. "A month is not long for courtship. I would suggest you make your choice quickly."

The unspoken threat hung heavy in the air. If he failed to take a bride, leadership of the company would pass to Hazim. The two men were rivals on the best days, enemies on their worst. And if his uncle took over leadership of the Adjalane Oil board that would mean an end to all the company's philanthropic pursuits— Hazim had made it perfectly clear he would divert all of the money in the budget earmarked for charity straight into plumping the company's bottom line. No new schools built. No more orphans rescued. No more hospitals constructed.

He looked each man sitting at the table in the eyes, seeing not even a hint of doubt in their eyes. They wanted him to marry? Fine. He squared his shoulders and stood. "I'll see you back here in a month, gentleman. With my American bride."

Get your copy of The Sheikh's Secret Bride from

www.LeslieNorthBooks.com

Made in the USA
Middletown, DE
10 June 2020